ISBN 978-0-578-50944-0

Contact Info Nanababymoore@gmail.com
Facebook- Shaniqua Moore

Shaniqua Moore

TABLE OF CONTENTS

Intro

Hello! my name is Shaniqua Moore for those who don't know but you can call me Nana. I don't know where the heck that name came from but that's what they call me (Laughing).

Born and raised in Rochester, Ny I'm 25 years old and been through more than the average person so I decided to open up my life to you all and hopefully my pain, my struggles and my life story can teach you all many lessons and help you get through life.

To all of my ex's starting from those I dated in high school all the way until now, all of you have a piece of my heart and I'm sorry for the pain I may have caused you.

To my best friends Pooh and Regg thank you for showing me what it feels like to have people in your life who genuinely cares for you despite your flaws.

To my family and my aunty Baldy thank you for showing me tough love even though y'all think I'm soft as fuck. Last but not least to my fans thank you all for the support it means everything and without y'all I am nothing. As you get into this book I need you all to know that My Karma is just the beginning of a pain free life. No need to feel sad or bad I want you all to feel happy and encouraged. Welcome to my life.

There He Was

There he was standing there brown skinned, pink lips, brush cut and his white ups on. I remember like it was yesterday. First day walking into high school not knowing anyone but somehow everyone knew who I was. As I walked down the hallway our eyes met for the very first time and he smiled at me but then a female approached him who had to be his girlfriend at the time.

Sitting in class across from him with this butterfly feeling that I just couldn't help but feel, but why? knowing he had a girlfriend so I stayed away. First day of school first crush and he have a girlfriend this can't be life.

∞ ∞ ∞

Two years passed now we are out of uniform and he is looking good as ever, waves spinning, muscles popping out his shirt and guess what? he was single (slight smile).

"Bitch guess who like you?"

Shaniqua Moore

"Girl who?" I asked

"That cute ass dark skinned boy that be with Ushawn." she said

"Oh!" not knowing who the hell she was talking about so I continued my day as I should then boom I run into him in the hallway and lord he was fine.

We exchanged numbers and that night we stayed on the phone until we had to be up for school. Remind you I didn't know anyone all I knew was that he was fine but I was young and he seemed a little older and more mature than me.

I wasn't sexually active at the time, but I could tell he was. My friends were all sexually active and me being that I became popular they swore I wasn't a virgin so to fit in I pretended that I wasn't.

We started getting acquainted and he became my first boo thing, the first guy I've ever loved, actually my first real boyfriend. We would do the normal boyfriend and girlfriend things like walk me to class, carry my books we kiss you know regular stuff. I didn't know much about being in a relationship I just knew I was happy and he was as well. Everyone warned me about him, they said that he was a hoe and he had fucked a lot of girls in the school but I didn't care because sex was the last thing on my mind and we really actually liked each other.

He was my Chocolate, dark skinned fine as ever and so sweet. Together for a while then one day he stopped calling me and coming to school and it felt like my world was over. Jail was the last thing on my mind and what do you know? his punk ass was in jail.

Heartbroken and sad because I've became attached to him, and even though I never told him I loved him and he never told me I knew deep down we had loved each other.

Finishing off my ninth grade year I was like to hell with relationships, then there he was. Standing at his locker and those butter-flies came right back.

∞∞∞

"Your name Nana?"

"Yeah why?" I asked

"Oh! I was just wondering because we were having a debate and they said you were the finest girl in the school". I smiled then I walked back to class.

A couple months later I haven't heard from my Chocolate and I felt maybe he just didn't wanna be with me anymore.

∞∞∞

"Hi" a soft voice coming from behind me. I turned around and there he was, the guy that I've been crushing on since 7th grade standing right there, I almost passed out. Calmly I replied

"Hey" he walked me to class that day and we became cool friends. We started spending all of our time together on the phone and sat next to each other in class and everyone assumed we were dating. We were though (Laughing) his soft lips and sexy body I used to love staring at that sexy face of his.

Hood Love

"Hi my Nana" he walked by and said

"Hi best friend you better call me tonight big ass ears" I responded

"Shut ya punk ass up for I drill you". We often flirted but nothing serious, he had a girlfriend and my crush and I were on and off but not together at the time.

I still haven't heard from my Chocolate so I was just having fun being a normal high school girl. Everyone thought we were together but we really weren't we just always used to drill each other, he was the class clown and so was I.

We used to be on the phone a lot so we kinda grew to like each other which wasn't my fault because if he wanted to be with his girlfriend he wouldn't have been calling me everyday.

School started getting intense because I would see him with his girl and he would walk down the hallway and smile at me and I roll my eyes and smile back. It was just something about his thug annoying ass. He used to get on my damn nerves but I was attracted to his hood ways.

∞∞∞

Sexy Face was beginning to stress me out. One minute we together then the next he wanna break up then be back together so I was just like whatever. The more I got to know Mr Hood he became a gentlemen and I seen sides no one would see. We begin to catch feelings for one another.

"I'm bout to just leave my girl and be with you" I didn't think he would actually do that until the next day in school he walked up to me and said "I did it". I was shocked like no you didn't. She walked down the hallway and I seen this sad look in her eyes but shit I didn't care but apart of me felt bad.

A year later we were still together his hood ass had me smiling from ear to ear, it's just something about them Westsiders. Mr Hood never asked me were I a virgin shit he was so weird I assumed his ass was too.

When everyone found out that we were officially a couple they were shocked, most people like what do you see in him and to him everyone felt like he had one of the baddest bitches in school. I used to love hearing him rap. He was so hood but so soft when it came to me.

I was his Booka and he was my Boo Bear. We got comfortable, the nigga took my virginity and his stupid ass didn't even know (laughing) and I didn't want him to know. Why? I don't know I kinda felt like I was too old to be a virgin.

We started fucking on the regular, arguing on the daily but still in love. Fighting in the hallways over only god knows what but his ass had turned me crazy and I never felt like that before, not even over Sexy Face or my Chocolate.

One day I came to school not thinking his ass would care about what my shirt said, because it had said "Almost Single" I walked in class and this girl says

"Ooooh you gone let her wear that shirt" he looked at me and choked me the fuck up when I tell you I was pissed I started swinging fast as hell but my arms just wouldn't reach his face for shit and then I flipped over the desk and we got kicked outta class. I never wore that shirt around his ass ever again (laughing). I still got that shirt til this day. That was my baby although the love we had was different.

He would piss me off over small things like I'll go on his Myspace and I'll be number one then he'll remove me lower like a bitch not paying attention so I would do the same. His stats would get to me so I would go to school and walk past him even though he would chase me and say "Don't get fucked up".

School dance coming up and we were still together we were just beefing at the time so me and my homegirls walked in looking cute and he was standing with his friends or whatever. Missing his touch but my pride was so big I refuse to show it and so was his.

"Bitch look at your boyfriend!" I looked over and this muthafucka had the nerve to be dancing with someone I thought was my homegirl I lost my mind, but still remaining calm.

Five minutes later he had the nerve to hit me in my head with a damn balloon, I punched him

in his face and just wouldn't stop swinging. My homegirls grabbed me and then his friends grabbed him. Just by looking in his eyes I knew that I had fucked up like Oh god this man is gonna kill me. Anger is what I seen from him for the first time ever but shit I ain't give a fuck you not about to just dance in my face and then hit me with a fucking balloon.

Next day it was a Saturday I get on Myspace and his stat had said "Just don't leave me" I was like "Aww he so cute" picked up the phone we talked, laughed and was right back together in love like nothing had ever happened. So to those that asked me "What do you see in him?" my response is "Everything".

Broken Heart

Chapter 3

Summertime is here and me and my bitches is out here turned the fuck up, but my cuffing ass was behaving though. I was still dating Mr Hood at the time so I would spend my days with my friends and then my nights with him.

"Bitch! it's hot as fuck out here let's go find some shade to sit in" Phone started ringing not recognizing the number I answered.

"Hello" I said

"Hey wassup I miss you" a deep voice responded

"Who is this?" as my heart begin to drop and tears formed in my eyes it was him my Chocolate. After all this time had passed it was my first time hearing from him. I sat there speechless wanting to ask so many questions but the words wouldn't form. Things like "Why?" How could you? Why me? but instead the phone said

"You have 60 seconds remaining". He said

"I'm sorry I went to jail now I live in Florida and I have to do my time here and before I could respond he said "I love you".

That was the first time he had ever spoken them words and before the phone hung up I replied "I love you too".

My friends were wondering who I was talking to but I never told them I just continued drinking my liquor and sat there speechless. Riding around and night time was approaching so we made our way to the westside,

"See you bitches tomorrow" I said and my home girl shouted

"Y'all have sex for me because my nigga ain't getting shit". We laughed and made our way in the house. I can smell the liquor and black & mild on his breath just knowing he's probably ready to have sex but I wasn't in the mood because of the phone call I had earlier that day.

Undressing me we started tongue kissing I grabbed his dick and he was aroused already, slowly climbing on top I rode him until we both came while thinking of my Chocolate the whole time. Feeling guilty and knowing things were about to change for the worse.

I started taking my anger out on him for no reason even though he wasn't doing anything wrong, I just needed some space to figure things out. Right before the summer was ending I called it quits. Ignoring his phone calls and his text's because deep down I still had hope for my Chocolate.

∞∞∞

I remember I logged on Myspace removed him from my top 8 and begin to look up my Chocolate page not thinking he had one. As my heart raced I went to his page and there you have it, he had a whole new born baby that I knew nothing about I cried, and cried and cried. Couldn't be, how? when? why? I've never knew what a broken heart had felt like but that night I was finally experiencing it.

Love Triangle

Single, walking into school the next year still hurting, depressed, not really wanting to run into any of my ex's but hey at least I was cute. Happy to see all my friends, new faces and new teachers.

There he was but still remaining calm (Sexy Face) trying not to give him any eye contact he walked by and smiled. I don't know what it was about him but my heart just melted whenever he would come around.

Every time we would breakup he never had a reason he would just say "It's not you, it's me". I never understood it but I had no choice but to respect it. Cheating never crossed my mind because he was such a great man, so I thought.

"Nani bitch I missed you!" my best friend had said

"Best friend bitch I missed you too let me see your schedule" we never had any classes together but somehow I always ended up in a class with Sexy Face or Mr Hood.

Walking into my first period class so many sexy boys I felt like a kid in a candy store but knowing I didn't wanna date no time soon.

Science class was lit no ex's no nothing just a handsome face with chinky eyes I had peeped but didn't pay too much attention to. Thirty minutes had passed and a knock from the door came, it was Sexy Face I damn near died. Like why can't I just have one class without seeing anyone from my past?

Staring out the corner of my eyes every second because lord he was fine but not wanting him to catch me so I wouldn't stare for too long. I would hear girls whispering asking about him saying stuff like he was fine but little do they know his ass was stuck on me just like I was stuck on him.

Funny because we never even had sex we just were somehow attached to each other. I thought his ass was a virgin (laughing) he was just so quiet but fine as he was I doubt it. Walking out of class a voice from behind me said

∞∞∞

"Hey can I walk you to your next class" I turned around and it was the boy I had peeped earlier. His style tight fitted clothing, fitted on and tattoos. I replied

"Sure" I knew my ex was looking but I was single so I didn't care but still knowing it made him jealous. Walking to my next class a few eyes on us that I had peeped but I smiled it off.

"You're so sweet thank you" I told him while giving him a hug

"Can I meet you right here and walk you to your next class?" he asked me

"Of course". I gave him a hug and walked in class.

Not focusing in class because I couldn't get my mind off my

Chocolate like you had a whole baby that I knew nothing about bothered the fuck out me. I left a good man thinking me and him had a future together but his bitch ass had started a future with only god knows who.

I would see Mr. Hood in the hallway but we never spoke we would just walk past each other. I had hurt him when he finally opened his heart to me so I didn't expect him to ever speak to me again.

Each day as time went on I found myself getting closer to Chinky Eyes. He was so sweet he would look at me and say "Poom Poom girl" don't laugh but it was cute.

A couple months had passed and he had told me he loved me. I wasn't ready for love so it left me speechless. Although I wasn't ready to say it back, I still stayed close to him. He would walk me home after school and we would sit at the park and just talk for hours. My family started liking him a lot but I just couldn't open my heart up to him for some reason. Next day we at school and everyone in my business trying to figure out if me and Chinky Eyes were dating but to me we weren't at the time, but to him we were.

After dating Mr Hood I wasn't used to being loved by a gentlemen. Maybe I was missing that hood love. I walked in class and my ex was sitting right there (Mr Hood) I was confused because first off that wasn't even his class so I felt he either wanted my attention or he was being funny. Apart of me wanted to walk out but instead I sat down and tried not to look up.

∞∞∞

"Booka" I heard him whisper from across the room. I ignored him but my heart smiled. I haven't spoken to him since we broke up so I was kind of surprised. "Booka" I had finally looked up and looked at him from across the room and all my feelings came back. His smile had made me smile, I still remember this day like it was yesterday . He had on a white t-shirt, a shirt wrapped around his head looking Muslim and light blue jeans.

"What?" I smiled and he whispered back

"I love you" it made me blush so hard to the point where my cheeks started hurting. Then the teacher told him to go to class. I sat there smiling the whole time after he had walked out.

∞∞∞

First period was over and guess who was standing there waiting? Chinky Eyes with that handsome face of his. His eyes never looked as if they were open which always made me laugh but he was so sexy though.

"Poom Poom girl I missed you!" he smiled and said

"I missed you too!". Later that night we talked on the phone and then I had a beep, it was Mr Hood calling. "Ima call you right back ok" I told him "you better ima be up waiting" he said *laughs*

"I am".

I switched over and me and him talked I even apologized for my actions that had taken place that summer and he had said that he forgave me. School wasn't as bad because we would speak in the hallways even though we weren't together but that was better than hating each other.

I started spending time with both of them without trying to get caught because for one I didn't belong to anyone and two I didn't wanna hurt anyone's feelings no more than I have. Chinky eyes was so sweet, I just wasn't ready to be loved by him and didn't know how to tell him that because his feelings for me were already strong.

∞∞∞

Life was becoming weird like where the hell all these men coming from? The timing was all wrong. I walked into the library and it was only one computer left and guess who was sitting next to it? Sexy Face. I didn't know if I should feel mad, happy, nervous or sad because I always loved him and couldn't let go and all he did was played with my heart and I couldn't figure out why. We sat there quiet I had on my headphones and he had on his. I remember he said something smart so I blurted

"What little boy?" he replied

"Ain't nothing little about me" I laughed and said,   "Oh really" while rolling my eyes without looking at him.

"Come over tonight and find out" I couldn't help but laugh like first off he so quiet and shy I never heard him talk like that and two I assumed he were a virgin but deep down this was someone I still was in love with but never had sex with and tonight was the night we were finally about to "do it". Should I go over or should I stay home had been on my mind that whole day but I had wanted to feel his touch, I wanted his lips against mine, I wanted him inside me.

Torn in between three guys that I had really cared for and broken hearted by one but thinking how long will I be able to keep this up? Butterflies in my stomach when I made it home I received a text.

"You coming over right" I replied

"Yeah **LITTLE** boy!" he hated that I would put "little" in front of everything.

"We gone see who little when you get here" I was nervous as

fuck not knowing what the hell I was getting myself into. I only had sex with one boy and that was Mr Hood so to me I felt like I didn't have that much experience but I had enough. I hopped in the shower got out and listened to my sex playlist while trying to get that nervous feeling out of my stomach. My heart raced the whole way to his house and plus my ass was tipsy which made me a little less nervous and more horny. I got out the car and text

"I'm outside" my heart was beating so fast I thought I was gonna have a heart attack. He opened the door and smiled. I followed him to his room and he turned on a movie and we laid down and watched half of it.

Next minute I know he got on top of me and we started tongue kissing. His lips were so soft I loved the way he kissed me. I can feel his manhood against my pussy which made me even more horny. My heart was beating fast but it felt as if his was beating faster. I was nervous but ready. The thought of having sex with the boy I've been crushing on since 7th grade, the boy who won't stop breaking my heart but the boy I can't let go.

He slowly eased my clothes off, I rubbed all my fingers across his 6 pack, I can tell he was nervous it was so cute. He went down on me I moaned softly while gripping the pillow until I came. He got on top and insert himself inside me. It felt so good almost magical, I dug my nails into his back and 4 strokes later he pulled out and came on his comforter set. I wanted to laugh so bad because it literally lasted 50 seconds. I can tell he was embarrassed but I thought it was cute.

I can hear my phone vibrating knowing it was either Mr Hood or Chinky Eyes but at the moment I didn't care about anyone else only him.

We rest for a while and round two we were back at it fucking for hours. I think he felt he had a point to prove (laughing). That nigga had me in every position and I loved each and every one of them.

Later that night I went home showered and looked at my phone I had a few missed calls from Mr Hood, Chinky eyes and my best friend had texted me. Not returning any of they calls because I was still shocked that my night was so perfect and unforgettable. I fell asleep happy but afraid because I still had to attend school the next day.

Mixed Feelings

That whole week of school had me stressed out trying so hard to avoid all three guys but it was impossible because I had a class with two.

Chinky Eyes would leave me long paragraphs on Myspace and I can tell Mr Hood wanted the relationship back but I knew it would hurt him if he found out I had sex with Sexy Face. My best friend thought it was hilarious but she didn't know I was actually scared. Scared to hurt someone.

I was out here doing whatever I wanted to do and not caring about anyone's feelings all because of a man that had a baby on me, a man who had hurt me. I wanted to call him or even message him on Myspace but I was afraid but more angry. Angry because he had to be out of jail and didn't tell me and I felt he could have told me he had a child. A child he had when we were together. I needed answers but not sure if I was ready for the truth.

My grades started slipping and my focus was no longer basketball. Leaving school I would go to this studio located near my house where I grew close to the owner and he became my big brother. I would tell him all about my problems and cry to him. Every relationship he knew about. Every song he knew who it was for. I remember I would walk down there even when I didn't want to make music and just get drunk and vent to him and no matter what he never judged me.

My friends knew most things but I never would tell them everything, why? Because no matter how much you think you can trust someone they'll use it against you when y'all are no longer friends. Hell it was five of us so I knew out the bunch one had to be disloyal even though I loved them so much.

I wanted to tell them about the night I had with Sexy Face but I waited because I knew they wanted me with Mr Hood and even though I loved Sexy Face deep down I knew I wanted to be with Mr Hood as well.

Chinky Eyes was adorable we still talked on the phone and I still let him walk me to class here and there but my mind was elsewhere. Who do I choose? am I ready to be in a relationship or should I just remain alone are all the questions that I would ask myself. Sexy Face was my everything but I was so tired of being dumped by him and taking him back so I kinda just cherished the sex we had and said whatever and a couple weeks later I was back with Mr Hood. Logging on Myspace I clicked on my messages and it was a long paragraph from Chinky Eyes. It made me cry, he said

"I hope you're happy with him, your smile is still beautiful as ever and even though it hurts to see you with someone else you'll always be my baby girl and I'll always love you Poom Poom girl. I'm gonna miss walking you to class and coming over after school I'm gonna miss you being mean to me lol and if he fuck up just know I'm right here waiting baby".

At the moment I knew I was becoming a heartbreaker and that one day karma would get me.

School wasn't the same just walking past Chinky Eyes and seeing that hurt in his eyes made me feel guilty. It's funny because I didn't realize how much he had meant to me until he no longer gave me his attention. I wanted his attention even if it was selfish. All the girls used to flirt with him in class and deep down it killed me but I couldn't say anything because I was back in a relationship.

One day I ran into him in the hallway and he asked for one last kiss even though I knew it was wrong, I was like hell I broke his heart I might as well give his ass this one last kiss. So we kissed and not thinking anyone was watching it got back to Mr Hood. I was furious when he asked me about the kiss but I didn't lie.

Everything went left the tension in the hallways was thick and everyone would notice. I didn't want them to fight each other because no one was wrong but me. Hell Mr Hood wasn't perfect but I stuck with his ass through his fuck ups to even though he never cheated well I don't believe he did but you just never know. Some people great at not getting caught.

Sexy Face never was into drama he would always mind his own business even when he would notice certain things. It all makes sense now that I think about it, he probably was doing him while I was doing me. I wanted sex from him once more but I didn't want the relationship, at least not at the moment.

∞∞∞

Everyone in school would laugh and say corny jokes like "Damn Nana I gotta get like you" or they would call me a heartbreaker it wasn't funny but at the time I was young and I didn't care as much.

One day I got the courage to text my Chocolate not knowing if he would reply I said

"Hey" he replied

"Who this?" I told him who it was and he pretended as if he had been trying to reach out to me but I doubt it because his ass could have looked me up on MySpace. He told me everything I needed to know and once again I was right the truth ended up hurting more than a lie ever will. I cried myself to sleep that night, I didn't even call my boyfriend because I just wasn't in the mood to talk to anyone.

End of the school year was approaching and I still kept in touch with them all while being in a relationship except Chocolate I didn't wanna talk to him at all after I found out everything I needed to know.

Sexy Face would text me here and there and ask me what I'm doing or he would send me a song and tell me go listen to it. I remember I would stop everything that I'm doing just to respond to his text. We never would actually talk on the phone which was cool because I was to shy when it came to him anyways.

I was beginning to have mixed feelings because I wanted something from all of them knowing it was impossible. I wanted that hood love from Mr Hood because when I was with him I felt safe and loved, I wanted Chinky Eyes compliments because he always made me feel beautiful, I wanted sex from Sexy Face and even though Chocolate had broken my heart apart of me still missed him but what do I do?

The Past

Chapter 6

For the rest of the year including the summer I kept Mr Hood as my man but kept the sex relationship with Sexy Face. Chinky Eyes had started dating again and I was happy for him. Somewhat jealous but still happy for him.

Me and my homegirls would turn up everyday of the summer at the studio and just have a ball with my brother Prestige. I was happy, I had a piece of Mr Hood and Sexy Face even though it was wrong. I kept Sexy Face around because after breaking Mr Hood heart the first time the relationship never really was the same and deep down it felt like there were other girls around. I could have been wrong or I could have been right.

Chinky Eyes and I stayed friends we would text every once in a while but nothing serious. I was getting used to doing whatever I wanted to do, coming home late and drunk every night, not answering my phone for anyone unless I was horny. I remember that summer I got a text that said

∞∞∞

"Can I ask you something?" it was from Chocolate I wanted to say

"Bitch no!" but instead I said

"Yes" he said

"Did you give my pussy away" I laughed before replying to his text and then I got angry. He knew that I was a virgin at the time and I always promised him that I would wait but hell I wanted him to hurt as much as he hurt me so instead of sending him paragraphs I responded

"Yes" while smiling. He told me he kind of figured because someone told him I was in a relationship. I can tell he was hurting. I was still hurting but I forgave him. I was through with the relationship but we remained friends. When the person you love have a baby on you, you never really heal your heart just adjust to the situation. I would go on his MySpace and stare at pictures of her and get sad because I felt that could have been us. He used to send me pictures of her I remember one time he did her hair and sent me a picture it made me smile. I always admired that he was a great father.

"I'll be back in Rochester this summer can I see you" not knowing how I would react or if I would cry, fight him, yell or scream I still wanted to see him. He came that summer and when I seen him all that anger had turned into hurt but I held back the tears and remained calm.

Grabbing me and holding me tight I laid on his chest and god did he smell good. I never wanted to let go. First time seeing him in years and it felt like the very first time when I saw him in the hallway.

"How you been? you looking good" without giving him eye contact I replied

"I'm alive so I can't really complain". He can tell I was starting to catch an attitude but I had to catch myself and smile it off. Not asking him how he been because if that bitch would of brought up his family I would have socked him. He was smart he kept the conversation about us.

Damn he was fine nice brush cut, waves spinning, teeth white and I still can remember his scent until this day. I asked

"What you about to get into?" he said "Look at you getting rid of me already" sure am for my nigga pop up his ass gotta go. I responded

"Won't you stop it's just me and my homegirls about to hang out and I don't wanna keep them waiting no longer than I have." After that day we kept in touch.

Self Love

S ometimes you gotta spend time with yourself and get to know who you are. They say hurt people, hurt people. Does that give you the right to go around treating people like crap? absolutely not.

Think back to that very first time when you've first experience a broken heart. All those nights you cried, stayed up tossing and turning, couldn't eat couldn't sleep and men this goes for you to. Think back to all those times when you tried to pretend nothing was wrong until someone finally asked "What's wrong?" and you broke down. Think back to all those nights while you were laid up with the next and you still couldn't take your mind off the way you were feeling.

 That same pain you experienced is that same pain we put people through and I don't wish that on my worst enemy. A broken heart hurts. It feels as if you can't breath your heart really aches. So before you go around hurting people think back to that same pain you once felt.

Why do hurt people hurt people? if you are one of those people who suffer from having family issues growing up, mental issues or maybe you were raped, molested, adopted, bullied, etc this chapter is for you. This chapter is for us.

Let go and let God. You gotta learn to forgive those people because if you don't it will turn you bitter. You don't jump from relationship to relationship to run from your pain you take time to yourself and get to know who **YOU** are. I didn't find myself until I was 23 and I'm 25 now and I never would have found myself if it wasn't for people hurting me, and me hurting people . I learned things about myself that I didn't even know about me.

See when you're around certain people and you have certain friends you do whatever it is to fit in. Never change who you are to please other people. It is not okay to go around hurting people. If you're not happy within you will not be happy in a relationship. That's why I say there is no better feeling than loving yourself.

Have you ever been hurt so bad it felt like you lost yourself, started dating again and then end up hurting the new person by going back to an ex? Understand this some people are meant to be left in the past, you could be missing out on the one who could have been for you.

The scariest part about love is wanting to go back to an ex thinking something will be different this time around even if you already taking them back for the 10th time. Apart of us still have hope but ask yourself do you love yourself if you keep letting the same person hurt you over and over?

Prom King

Chapter 8

School was back and Mr Hood & I relationship wasn't the same. We argued every other day but we just didn't wanna breakup. Something about him I can never figure out. He was an asshole to the world but soft and gentle when it came to me.

We would argue in school and he'll text me and tell me meet him in the hallway and when I met him he would be standing there looking me in my eyes as if I meant everything to him.

Sometimes I wanted to cry because the way he looked at me was so genuine and I would be so mean to him because I knew I didn't deserve him. I didn't deserve his love. I constantly pushed him away and the more I did the harder he fought to keep me around.

That was my baby. I knew I had to get my shit together before I lost him forever. When it comes to having a good man he was that and if his heart was to never wanna love again I know deep down I would be the blame.

Me and Chocolate stayed friends but for some reason I couldn't stop messing with Sexy Face. I wanted them both. It's like this guy had a spell on me since when I first saw him in 7th grade.

That whole school year was getting intense, every time Mr Hood pissed me off I would spend more time with Sexy Face and when Sexy Face pissed me off I'll be right back under Mr Hood.

We had broken up before prom and I was back in a relationship with Sexy Face but already had prom plans with Mr Hood. I had explained to Sexy Face that we already had agreed to go to prom and he understood so he let me go. I knew he wasn't going to prom anyway. He agreed that I can go to fast not paying it any attention I said "Cool".

Me and my friends were so excited I was kind of sad I wasn't going with my man instead I was going with my ex who I knew I had still loved. So guess what I did? I asked my best friend to join us so that way it can be a date with three instead of just me and him.

While getting ready for prom that week me and my bitches knew we were gonna be the talk of prom.

I loved my friends but the love I had for my best friend was pure. She was my rider, my heart whenever I needed her she came, and nothing could come & between that. When y'all seen me y'all seen her we never left each other's side. She was my backbone, I was the nice friend and she was the turn up I'll beat a bitch ass friend.

Sai asked,

"Who are you going to prom with pink lips?"

"Bitch shut up!" I laugh so loud when he said that but ignored his question and went and took my material for my prom dress. I just knew that purple was gonna look so outstanding on me.

Sitting in class the next day I asked can I use the bathroom so I walked out the door and when I came in the hallway my man "Sexy Face" was on the phone and hurried up and hung the phone up when he saw that I had noticed. Following behind me

I couldn't help but wonder who he was on the phone with but I never asked.

When it came to him I had become soft, I would never curse around him, raise my voice or even try to argue with him and I never knew why. I was blinded by his looks but one day I was gonna find out who the mystery person he was on the phone with.

∞∞∞

Prom was here, it came so fast I wasn't even ready and my dress wasn't back. I went to the hairdressers and fell in love with my hair but I was running out of time.

"Who doing your makeup?" my hairdresser had asked

"No one" I replied she said

"Wait a minute I'll be right back" she went in the back room and came back with makeup. When I tell you she had me looking so beautiful I couldn't believe it. She gave me some lip gloss and it was lit.

Rushing to get my dress now I'm two hours late for prom thank god I had showered before I left. My phone was going off like crazy and I knew it was Mr Hood and my best friend calling. I get there and guess what? My dress wasn't done. I panicked, sat there for 30 minutes before she gave it to me. I rushed home put my dress on looked in the mirror and couldn't believe my eyes.

My family was so shocked I looked so gorgeous my butt looked big an I was ready to get the hell out of the house. Sai and I took some pictures and so did a few of my other cousins then I was out the door. I didn't know how to walk in heels so I pretended I did that day. Not knowing how to drive my cousin had to pick up my best friend and my ex Mr Hood.

I made it to his house and almost died, he was standing there looking so damn sexy, his hood ass was wearing the fuck out that tux. We were shy his family had asked to take pictures of us and he grabbed me and smiled, butterflies is what I felt while smiling from ear to ear trying to get Sexy Face out my head just for the day but I couldn't.

Rushing to pick up my best friend because we were damn near missing prom. When we made it there everyone face dropped. I walked by feeling like the baddest bitch in the school.

"That's Nana damn she looking good as fuck",

"Omg Nana you look so beautiful" I wanted to say "Bitch I know" but I smiled and said thanks while walking by. Funny how the same females who didn't like me gave out the most compliments and their boyfriends eyes were glued on me the whole night.

Mr Hood had went off and partied with his friends while I partied with mine. I text Sexy Face probably twice that night to let him know that I had missed him then after that the liquor had kicked in. I had forgot I had a boyfriend (laughing)

"This is for all my lovers in the building tonight" the Dj announced and then Dru Hill "I love you" came on. Our eyes met and he made his way to me, pulling me close we slow danced and all eyes were on us.

Heart beating fast I felt like his woman again. Next song came on and it was Beyoncé "Dangerously In Love" he grabbed me tighter and the words Beyoncé Sang "I can't do this thing called life without you here with me" made tears come down my face I couldn't hold back what I was feeling for him anymore, I wanted my man back. My eyes were closed but I can see the flashes from people's cameras in my face and I heard someone say

"Aww she's crying they are to fucking cute" I didn't care

that I had cried the emotions were strong and I couldn't fight it anymore. His eyes were watery but he hid his well.

"Booka you know I love you right" my voice had cracked I couldn't respond so he said it again "You know I love you right" I nodded my head. He said

"Stop crying everything will be ok and then he wiped my face".

Prom was over and when we made it outside it was pouring rain,

"Huh take my jacket" I wanted to hell my hair was popping but I said "No give it to my best friend" then we all ran to the car. We ended up going out to eat I felt my phone vibrating, then reality kicked back in. My boyfriend text and ask how was prom. I wanted to say

"Nigga the shit was lit, I'm looking good as fuck and I got my man back what's really good" but I wasn't that brave so I text back

"It was okay I guess, I miss you though". Sitting at the table eyelash hanging from me crying I didn't care I had so much fun. I knew I wanted my relationship back that night but I wanted to wait until the morning to talk to Sexy Face.

Mr Hood sitting there with his crown on because he had won Prom King of course I wasn't gonna win the whole school hates me but he looked good as fuck in it. I wanted to fuck him while he wore it.

The drinks started kicking in and I can tell he was drunk and horny. I already had felt bad for making out with him at prom knowing I was in a relationship but everything just felt so real.

We end up leaving The Distillery and going to this hotel gathering for an hour but when my best friend said she was leaving I knew I was ready to go as well.

"You coming with me" Mr Hood whispered in my ear" my pussy said yes but my mouth said "No I'm sorry I'm sleepy". I wasn't sleepy I just already was feeling guilty for kissing him and fucking him would have been even more worse. He was furious, and I understood why but if he loved me, he would have understood my reasons.

I ended up going home that night by myself and when I tell you my night was worth it, it was worth it, but out of that whole night if I could have changed one thing I would have....

Torn

Chapter 9

The next day I woke up to 50 missed calls and text messages from my boyfriend. I knew something was wrong so instead of calling him I read his texts.

"You must think I'm an ass!" my eyes got big as fuck I text him and said

"What are you talking about?" he said

"I seen the pictures from prom got me out here looking stupid my homeboy showed me all of them. I wanted to say well "Did ya little homeboy tell you before we got back together me and him went to the movies and seen Avatar but ended up missing the movie because we were too busy making out" but I shut up.

Rushing to Myspace to see what pictures he was talking about and there they were me in my ex arms kissing him and you can see the tears running down my face in the picture. Like first off you hating bitches would post something on the internet without telling me first but whatever. Now he knows how I felt every time he would breakup with me for no reason.

"I know you fucked him!" he said

"First off all we did was kiss and that was it I went home alone".

"I'm supposed to believe that shit!" he texted back. I can tell he was angry because he never cursed before or at-least at me.

He had pissed me off I swear if I could rewind time I would have fucked Mr Hood on prom night, and I would have fucked him good. That's my only high school regret. This boy had the nerve to be so fed up and done but he only got one up on me because I can never catch him doing dirt. He had to be doing something I don't believe in perfect.

We end up breaking up and after that I posted the rest of the pictures from prom that I wanted to keep just for me. Them pictures were so beautiful they probably still on Myspace.

I wanted that school year to end so bad I never wanted to run into him again. Everything was different and here came the drama. I walked into school that Monday and it felt as if all eyes were on me. Something wasn't right I get to my locker and a girl smiled at me.

The fuck this bitch looking at. Her and my ex had called each other "Brother and sister" so I knew she had something to do with it because she never liked us together. I snapped   "What the fuck is you smiling at?" I yelled "Ah you mad because he dumped you" she blurted back.

"Fuck him and those dead ass flowers I got tired of him buying" my friends grabbed me and calmed me down.

Sitting in class pissed off not wanting to be there. If he would have walked in that class room while I was angry I probably would have smacked the church out of him. He never seen me angry before and he was about to witness a side I never wanted him to see. I was ok with us breaking up because I didn't want his ass anymore anyway but when you out here saying only god knows what and making it seem like I was out here hurting you is another issue for me. I was down for him every time he broke my heart, each time he left me and came back even started dating one of my cousins and yet I was still there with open arms but I can only blame myself for being a fool for him.

Walking down the hallway and this bitch bumped me, I lost my mind and flipped out she got on her phone and called another girl out of class but I was ready to fight, Chinky Eyes grabbed me.

"Don't touch me!" I yelled at him.

"Baby you have to calm down it's not worth it" we broke up forever ago and this man still calls me baby to cute, but anyways I got sent home that morning.

I came back to school that afternoon calm and these bitches tried me again now I'm suspended and my best friend and my squad was war ready. I don't know who told them what had happened but they were pissed and ready to ride.

∞∞∞

Sitting home suspended and mad because I haven't ran into Sexy Face because he knew better and mad because I'm the only one who got suspended. I called my girls up and we end up going to the beach.

"Sis (K-naste) wassup baby who you here with?" happy to see her I gave her a hug.

"My brothers them here and Tierra here she at the pier," she said. I found all my friends and we walked around looking cute trying to take my mind off school.

Thirty minutes later we end up running into them, I tried to avoid it but the next minute I know they went and got thirty people and came walking towards us. My homegirl said

"Well give Nana the round or one of you bitches give me the round" everyone got quiet and all that tough mess that was going on in school disappeared. A lady that was with them asked did I live on Scio and was my mother name Crissy I said yes she said

"How would your mama feel if she knew you were out here about to fight? stop all that mess we all like family and life is to short you're too pretty to be out here fighting y'all should be ashamed of y'all self". She talked to me for about an hour and as I looked out the corner of my eye my best friend was rolling her eyes.

I knew she wanted to fight all of them because the love she had for me was ride or die type and she felt my heart was pure and that I forgave people to easily. It was getting dark and a lot of fights were starting to break out then we heard gunshots and went home.

Mr Hood text me that night and asked was I ok. We talked about prom and I was back on cloud nine.

My friends had my back that night and that's why no matter the distance if they call me today I'll still be right there for them. We were all in the 11th grade but this was my best friend last year in high school and I was sad because I was going to have to go through a whole year of school without her.

Fool For Him

Chapter 10

"**B**itch remember them gunshots we heard at the beach, why it was that boy Booka who got killed".

My best friend and I talked about that whole night she was angry that I handled the situation different she was ready to fight everyone.

I get to school and Sexy Face was in the lunchroom standing next to that bitch so I walked passed both of them and sat down. Y'all don't know how bad I wanted to choke slam his ass off that table. It's like I loved him and hated him at the same time.

Mr Hood and I were cool but not close how we used to be. I'm sitting down mad at the world and I can see Mr Hood best friend throwing food our way.

"If this muthafucka hit me with something swear to god I'm going to snap" before I could finish talking shit a carrot hit me right in my forehead. I was so embarrassed and already pissed because I was having a bad day. I looked across the room and everyone was laughing. I went towards him and he started running and laughing. I went back to the table where my homegirls were and we mixed different foods inside of this milk carton and I carried it until I ran into him then boom there he goes standing next to Mr

Hood.

I walked over to him and poured it all over him. I could tell he probably wanted to fight me but I didn't care he shouldn't have hit me with a carrot. He yelled

"Bro swear to god you better get this bitch for I slap her!" My ex started laughing and said "That ain't got shit to do with me" he took his shirt off and continued cursing me out like he wanted to get in my face but deep down I wasn't worried and he low key had a crush on me well we both liked each other but that was before I dated his best friend.

Walking into class I see Sexy Face sitting down so I sat there for 5 minutes and then asked the teacher can I use the bathroom knowing I wasn't coming back. As I go into the hallway I see Mr Hood best friend still pissed standing in the hallway by himself in my head I'm like fuck why do I have to run into him? This time around it wasn't an angry look it was more of a sad look.

"Really Nana, man why you do that? I thought I was ya boy" he said sadly.

"I'm sorry but you really made me mad" we apologized to each other and then afterwards we started laughing. I couldn't stand his big headed ass but his sense of humor made me like him I just never wanted to date him.

∞∞∞

I ended up going home early that day I just wasn't in the mood to be in school. I looked at my phone and it was a text from Sexy Face that said R Kelly "I can't sleep" so I went on youtube and listened to the song.

Tears begin to run down my face. I wanted to be done with him for good but my heart wouldn't let me, I wanted him and I needed him.

"That song was cute" I replied

"I miss you can you come over so we can talk when I get out of school he asked"

"Okay" I text back. I knew if my friends would have found out we were even holding a conversation they would be pissed but I didn't care. I went to his house and we talked and ended up having makeup sex.

His dick was so good that I was blinded by the love. We started back sharing lockers and his fake sister was pissed I laughed and smiled her way.

Turning around I see my best friend standing there with the rest of the girls

"So this what we doing now? you choosing this weak ass nigga over us bitch fuck outta here every time he broke your heart you cried to me fuck him you don't need him!". All eyes were now on us I stood there speechless because she was right but the way she went about it wasn't.

Without saying anything I closed my locker and we continued walking to class.

"Why she mad at you?" my homegirl Nisha asked. "Girl because she don't want me with him" walking up the stairs as I'm explaining the story to her I run into my best friend again but this time she was angry as if she wanted to fight. So I stopped walking and approached her.

"It's really not that deep y'all making a scene in the hallway all for what y'all corny for that". I understood why my best friend was mad but when I saw the rest of my groupie ass Charlie's Angels looking ass home girls acting like they wanted to fight me as well I got heated.

The sentry broke us up and sent us to class. Logging on to Myspace I see a post from my best friend and the rest of my friends talking about me. I put my head down and I cried. The teacher asked me was I ok and I asked can I leave the class and she had said yeah. I got my stuff out of my locker and went home.

I had told my family what had happened and they were upset because they always told me my loyalty to them would backfire one day and it did. I went to my room and cried some more and then the pain had turned me angry I logged on MySpace and wrote post after post talking shit and that day I knew our friendship was over for good. School was ending and right before graduation I found out Mr Hood had went to jail.

My Advice

Chapter 11

L ove hurts, but love is a beautiful feeling when everything is going just fine. No matter how many times
you get hurt, love like no one has ever hurt you before and keep
your friends and your family out of your business.

When you're in a relationship no one should know what
you're going through but you and your partner. If you go to your
friends or to your family telling them about the person you're
with and how they're hurting you they're not gonna be okay with
that. You're making them not like this person and it's all because
they love you and don't wanna see the next person hurt you. We
can't tell the next person how bad someone is treating us because
when you get back in a relationship with that person our friends
and family aren't going to accept them and we can't get mad.

Just learn to keep people out of your business. Communi-
cation saves relationships and friendships.

If you care about someone pick up the phone and talk it out, you
don't run to the internet to hurt each other's feelings. Pride is
one hell of a drug. My whole high school experience was a lesson
learned. I've broken hearts and had mines broken, I lost the person
who meant most to me my best friend, my rider, my hitta, and as

you read this book it's been 8 years and I still haven't apologized. I'm sorry from the bottom of my heart. (You know who you are) and to my high school lovers I hope you all find it in your hearts to forgive me. If it's meant maybe I'll run into you after high school (smiling) or am I? Who knows just keep reading this book and y'all might find out more.

Senior year

L ast year of high school, nervous but excited. Like damn who the hell Ima hang with this year? Yeah I had associates but I was beginning to miss my girls. Some had graduated and some was still there but the bond was gone.

Me and Sexy Face was broken up as always and I didn't care at the time. My last year of school I just wanted it all to be over. I still thought his ass was sexy though. Every time he walked passed me in the hallway I wanted to die but I had to stop messing with him because the love was beginning to hurt but at the same time felt so good. I knew he had a girlfriend because that's the only time when he will cut me off. I didn't show that I was bothered but I was. I was missing his touch, his soft gentle kisses or maybe I just missed the sex because his ass wasn't shit.

Mr Hood was still in jail I felt bad for him and thought of him every once in a while. School wasn't the same neither was out of it. Life had changed for the worse when I lost my best friend.

Before my senior year I would spend my summer days in the house because I had no one to hang with. I was depressed no friends no relationship it was just me. I would sit in the house and blast slow music just to annoy Sai and Baby C.

"Nana get out the house all miserable and shit you and your bestie bugging y'all both miss each other so just call her with your little ass head".

"Bitch shut up! I'm not depressed" he replied "You are all you do is listen to slow music and be emotional all the time you too damn emotional".

I shut my door and laid in bed because I knew he was right. I also knew she had missed me as well because we had mutual friends who would tell me every time she drinks she would bring up the memories we shared. It made me smile but also sad. I just knew school wasn't going to be the same and I was right. I had no one to flirt with how boring is that.

Chinky Eyes fine ass had stopped coming to school and when he would come he didn't stay long. I didn't even wanna talk to him I just liked to secretly stare at him. He was fine as hell. Whenever he saw me he would give me the biggest hug and say

"I love you Poom Poom girl". It was always our insider. One of my nicknames is "Poom Poom" and no one in school knew but him and he knows I hated that name but the way he would say it always made me blush.

I had a new group of associates that I would hang with but I wouldn't get to close because I just didn't trust females anymore. My senior year was okay school went by fast next minute I know prom was coming up.

I decided not to go. Me and Sexy Face was on talking terms but I still felt someone else was in the picture so I kept my distance. Everyone went except me. I kinda wished that I had did just so I can show off one last time and walk in looking like a snack. After prom I came back to school and my homegirl was like

"Bitch they was in there taking pictures with your man" I started laughing

"Girl that is not my man"

"No Nana but still it's a respect thing if we all hang together". I felt some type of way but apart of me like whatever bitches ain't shit, he ain't shit and I ain't shit.

I enjoyed the rest of the school year we went to sea breeze with the school and they got me high for the first time. I was so damn high I stared out that window our whole ride there laughing about absolutely nothing. I wasn't a smoker but the feeling just made me feel good.

The whole time I was there I got on one ride and damn near died. It took my friends thirty minutes to convince me to get on this ride and when I finally sat in that seat reality kicked in. I jumped up so fast to hop off that shit and scratch myself in the face and started bleeding. It felt like I was having an anxiety attack I was sweating and paranoid. I watched Final Destination way to many times and I couldn't go out like that.

Just when I got up my friends told the man to hurry and start the machine and he did as they said. When I tell y'all I died, I died, that damn ride took us in the air and just dropped I yelled for dear life my friends thought it was absolutely funny but I didn't. I was damn near on the floor holding on for life asking god to please get me off safe. I looked at my homegirl Tiff and said

"Bitch we bout to die" she had tears in her eyes she wouldn't stop laughing so it made me laugh. At the time it wasn't funny but now that I think about it I behaved like a ten year old. I do not like getting on rides and probably never will get on one again. I don't know if it was because I was high as fuck or what but it scared me for life.

We got off that ride and I stopped talking to everyone because I was mad but they didn't care they still were laughing. My face was cut because I had accidentally scratched myself trying to get off then eventually I just started laughing then we sat down and ate.

Sexy Face kept texting me asking me what I'm doing and was I having fun, dry texting him back because I know he didn't care he just probably needed someone to text because for some reason he didn't want to come.

∞∞∞

Graduation was coming up and I was so happy I was stress free and finally about to get out of that stressful ass school. Two weeks before graduation I had forgave Sexy Face and we were right back dating.

Deep down I had felt he changed or maybe I was just a sucker when it came to his love. A lot of people didn't agree with us being back together but I didn't care we only had a few weeks left of school anyway. Walking down the hall I started seeing new faces and one face stood out.

"Damn he fine" but who is he? I seen my homegirl talking to him and I wanted to ask but I waited. I was going to find out one day.

Few weeks passed and graduation came up, I went and got me a cute dress and some heels to go under my cap and gown. Walked in and seen all my homegirls I was excited, sad but happy we were finally walking the stage and most of all I was walking the stage with the love of my life. The boy I had a crush on since 7th grade, the boy who broke my heart a thousand times but the boy I just couldn't seem to let go.

They called his name before mines and I jumped out of my seat and yelled "That's my baby" I was so happy I couldn't control myself. Then they called mine, as I walked to the stage I was thinking should I crip walk and throw up the east side or keep it classy, I kept it classy though (laughing).

I heard my family yelling it made my heart smile I did it I finally graduated, all that pain hurt, tears, & happiness, was worth it.

After graduation we took pictures outside, my family wanted to go out to eat and so did his family and sad as it sounds I went with his family. I just wanted to be with him. We sat and ate and he had asked me to come over, probably because I was looking good in my dress and he was looking good to.

 We never actually had many deep talks but he apologized for putting me through hell and my punk self forgave him. We tongue kissed for ten minutes he slowly took my dress off, went down on me until I came, tongue kissed me some more and then slid inside me. The way we made love that night I just knew I wanted to spend forever with him. It felt like we were making love for hours. Time had passed and it was damn near three in the morning so I stayed the night. I'll never forget graduation.

Life After High School

No More waking up for school and damn it felt good. My homegirl had given me thousands of pictures to have, some of me and her but plenty of others.

I got to a picture of my man and he was looking so fine on prom but an unfamiliar face was standing near him spraying something that looked like oil sheen on his hair, why? Who the hell knows but I assumed it was a family member so I brushed it off. Every picture made me smile some even made me sad.

After high school not everyone stay close but if I didn't learn anything else I learned to never play with people's hearts and to never turn your back on your friends.

I remember getting on Facebook and I seen the fine ass boy from night school page so I sent him a friend request just to be nosy then my phone vibrated

"Hey babe I miss you come over" it was Sexy Face I got dressed quick as hell because he work so much but I wanted all of his time. When I made it there he was sitting there all sexy on his bed with his muscles out I was ready to have sex hell I was tipsy to. So we ended up having sex, rough sex throwing it back while he smacked my ass while I looked back at him.

After we got done he got up and went downstairs, his phone went off. I told myself nope I'm not gonna look because when you go looking for dirt you break your own heart. My stupid ass looked anyway and it was a text from a girl that read

"Why do you keep hurting me like this? I really love you" my heart dropped I sat there angry, he seen it in my face when he came back into the room. I wouldn't say nothing he grabbed his phone and his face frowned up as if he was surprised. He walked over to me and I yelled

"Don't fucking touch me!" as tears ran down my face. I was hurt because I figured whoever this person is gotta be the same girl that was there all along. He wouldn't let me go, he had seen the hurt in my face so instead of leaving me alone he undressed me and made love to me.

I was still angry, upset and hurt and the tears wouldn't stop flowing. I had loved him more than I love myself and that was my biggest fear. Every time he broke my heart I allowed him to come back because I only wanted him. He got off me and walked out the room and my phone went off. It was a text from him that said

"Just leave me" instantly becoming angry because he had to walk out the room to send a text all because he was guilty and had flipped it as if I had done something wrong. I called my homegirl and cried like never before on my way out of his house, he asked for a hug I ignored him and walked off.

I remember crying for days then he finally texted me and said

"I'm sorry I can't do this anymore" like first off how you break my heart twice? what is this the breakup remix? Not being over the text message that I had read then to breakup with me like I had done something wrong was a pain that I had never felt before.

I couldn't eat, sleep or think. I wanted to die. Why me? I had given him my all I loved him with everything in me and all he ever done was hurt me and I just couldn't understand why and the scariest part about it all was that if he were to come back I would have allowed him.

New Beginnings

Chapter 14

Depression was starting to kick in, I had stopped going outside, eating and making music I just wanted to be left alone. I was hurting bad and even more hurt because I knew he didn't care.

We had never gone this long without talking before so maybe we were done for good this time. Slowly but surely I was finding myself again, I had left social media for months and started back going to the studio spending most of my time there. That was my happy place, whenever I went around my big brother all my sadness would go away. We would sip wine or sometimes drink liquor and just vibe to music all day.

I was missing my friends but my pride was still high. Why do we hurt the ones that love us the most? Apart of me needed answers this was someone I've been in love with since 7th grade and the shit just won't go away. Maybe my karma was catching up to me.

As the days begin to pass my heart started to beat regularly again. I finally was eating, going to the gym and I activated my Facebook back. Everyone had missed me and asked where I have been, I just pretended that I took a break to focus on my music. I guess that's better than telling them what was really going on because a lot of people on facebook had looked up to me and felt I was their role model. Afraid of letting them down I held everything in. I never understood why I was the voice to a lot of people that I came in contact with throughout my years whether it was through social media or in person. Maybe because deep down most new my heart was pure and that my intentions were always good even when I made mistakes at times.

∞∞∞

"Nana let me get some candy I'll give you a dollar" I jumped up quick and tried to lock my room door before Sai can enter my room. I looked on my dresser and noticed that some were missing which had to be him who had taking it.

Now Sai was that older cousin who you go to for everything, who you look up to and wanna be just alike. I loved him so much like a big brother but for some reason I just liked giving him a hard time. Opening my door quick he smiled and said

"Please I got you" I can hear his best friend laughing in the next room. Before I could answer he took it and closed my door back.

That morning I got up and turned my music on as Beyonce "Cater to you" played loudly through the speakers.

"Nana turn that up that's my shit" Sai yelled from the next room. I laughed and did as he said.

"Yo know funny shit that bitch can sing". Sai was one of them hood dudes that you just can't picture listening to slow music like Beyonce so whenever I would play certain songs and hear him singing it made me laugh so hard.

A year has passed and I was out of high school with nothing to do, no friends, no boyfriend, no one I could even creep with so I would scroll down my timeline on Facebook all day.

A familiar face had popped up on my page, he had on a black durag with his shirt off looking good as fuck. Where do I know him from? Clicking his page I started reading his comments and seen one of my homegirls write something under it.

"The boy from night school" I said out loud. I remember walking passed him a few times in the hallway when I was going to class trying to figure out who he was. Still being nosy I went through every last picture and didn't see one female in neither of them. He was fine I wanted to get to know him but I didn't wanna reach out to him first. I liked a few of his pictures then I clicked off his page and took a nap

∞∞∞

"Nana bring your little dike ass outside and have a drink" I lived with my aunty my whole life she was more like a mom to me even though my mom had lived next door to her. I laughed and yelled out my window

"Bitch here I come with your ugly ass!" See me and her have this bond that no one will ever understand we play all day like friends but I love my aunty to death. Throwing on my shorts I went downstairs.

"Crissy you have one ugly ass daughter" Crissy was my mom the cool mom that everyone just love and I wouldn't trade her for the world.

"Leave my baby alone you're something else". Handing me my drink we sat outside as I blast slow music out my window. It was summer time so our house stayed with a lot of company.

Sometimes I would catch myself daydreaming and thinking of Sexy Face because I was still hurting it's like the more I drank the sadder I became.

Logging on Facebook I go to my messages and my heart lit up, it was the boy from night school who had inbox me it said

"Hey wassup" I read it four times before I could reply. Smiling as I replied

"Hey" I wanted to write so much more at the time but I didn't wanna seem thirsty so I played it cool.

"Do you wanna talk on the phone," he wrote back, deep down I was very shy and I would rather talk through messenger or talk through texting but he wasn't going for it. I waited 30 minutes waiting for the liquor to kick in so I wouldn't be as shy then I called.

"Hello is this so and so" we talked for hours that night and for the first time my mind was off of Sexy Face and it felt great. I told him I do music and play basketball and he stopped me and said

"So what you telling me is that you're nice and you can beat me" I laughed and said

"I'm almost positive that I can beat you"

"So how about we make a bet if I beat you, you have to treat me to ice cream and if you beat me I have to treat you to ice cream". I wanted to say shit

"If you beat me I'll give you some pussy and if I beat you I'll still give you some pussy. (Laughing) the liquor was starting to kick in but I kept my cool and said

"Yes that sounds like a plan" we talked for about five hours that night before hanging up. I had liked him he seemed different from the rest but I wanted just a friendship at the moment and

Shaniqua Moore

nothing more.

Daddy's Little Girl

Chapter 15

I always wondered what it felt like to be daddy's little girl. I wanted that bond that some females have with their fathers, talks about what men to stay away from you know the stuff females are supposed to hear from home.

Sometimes I ask myself is this why I am the way I am? Angry, lost, and running into the same no good ass men.

I remember when I was young my dad would give me everything I asked for, he remembered my birthday and always made sure he told me happy birthday while handing me $200 dollars in a white envelope.

Deep down I didn't want that I wanted his love and his time. As I got older it's like he forgot to tell me happy birthday or I would have to remind him the same day but he remembered all my other siblings birthdays.

I used to cry because when it came to my mother kids I felt he didn't care as much as he cared about my other sisters and brothers. I would get on Facebook and he would post their pictures and tell them happy birthday just hoping one day I would see me on his page but I never did.

Why me? is it something I did wrong to make him not wanna show how much he loves me because I know he does. I keep it to myself but there are some things I want to ask him.

There are so many times I let men walk all over me, cried myself to sleep, went days without eating and I just wanted my dad love. I'm 25 and I only could remember hugging him two times in my life and I have no pictures with him. Everyone else got pictures with him except me.

Me and my dad are just alike, I'm shy and he's very quiet himself it's like the only time we talk is when I have a question about music or I need a few dollars. Maybe if I got that love from him I would know my worth.

This chapter is for my ladies who doesn't have that love from their fathers or maybe never even met their father. You are strong, beautiful, intelligent and most importantly god's creation because he makes no mistakes. Don't let the lack of love that you received from your father be the reason you miss out on good people in your life.

Don't let that be the reason you sleep with just any man, be smart and cherish your body. Know your worth queen.

My Man

Mr Unpredictable was everything I've ever wanted in a man. He used to make me feel beautiful, special and like a queen. We took our relationship very slow and started off as friends first. I knew everything about him and he knew everything about me.

"Good morning my love can I see you today?" logging on facebook every morning was the exact same message. The first time we ever actually chilled in person was at this park near my old neighborhood boy was he fine. He had on a black du-rag a black shirt and some big ass jeans. I was so shy I couldn't even look him in his eyes. The females in the neighborhood would walk past us like

"Aww Nana is that your boyfriend he cute" he wasn't my man at the time but I knew he would be so I just told them all yeah.

"Oh! so I finally got the title now" he laughed and picked me up and kissed me for the first time. I closed my eyes and enjoyed it then he put me down and gave me a hug. We sat at the park talking until it was like 3 in the morning.

"Nana come here" my cousin whispered softly so I came.

How you know him? do you know I was at this party with

him and his brothers and they raped this girl" my heart dropped to my feet I didn't know what to believe because my cousin lie so much and I felt the rumor just couldn't be true. She walked away so I shyly walked back over and sat down.

"What's wrong are you okay?" he asked, yes I replied.

"I know that girl that you were talking to from somewhere"

"That's my cousin she was just saying the same thing about you" I replied without telling him the full details. An hour later another female from the neighborhood had pulled me to the side and said

"Wasn't he in the newspaper for raping someone" that was it I couldn't hold back anymore so I walked over to him, by then the park was clearing up and it was just us three outside.

"Is there anything you wanna tell me"?

"No my love why?"

"Because people keep saying something about you and your brothers raping someone please don't lie to me just tell me the truth". He ended up cursing the girl out and she walked home and then he explained the situation. If my man tell me he's innocent then he's innocent. He admitted to being at the party but then he explained that the girl was lying and never even seen his face because he wasn't there long.

Later that night we talked for a few more hours then he walked home I felt bad because it was so late at night and I didn't know he stayed that far away. He called me when he made it home I was happy that he was safe and thirsty to hear his voice because I had missed him already.

Logging on my computer, I decided to look up his name, heart beating fast and there it was his face all over the website but I took a deep breath and told myself my man is innocent and I would always defend him and stand by his word.

What If

Chapter 17

"I wanna take you out to eat today where do you wanna go?"

"Friendly's" I replied. We went to Friendly's almost every week, that had eventually became our favorite restaurant. I still remember exactly what we both used to order.

After we ate I went back to his house, afraid because I had never met his mother I walked in and everyone spoke. One of his brothers went to high school with me and the other one had just ask for my number on Facebook but I ignored him, thank god I did because that would have been awkward.

Following him straight to his room I sat on the edge of his bed how us females sit when we be fake shy (laughing). I examined his room, looking on his mirror there were nothing but pictures of Alicia Keys. He was a very clean person and I loved that about him. He came back in the room and said

"You fine and all but no jeans on in my bed" I laughed like oh he think he slick, while removing my clothes and laid down next to him. We listened to slow jams while kissing for ten minutes. In my head I just knew what was about to happen next, it had been awhile since i've had sex but I had made him wait so long I figured tonight would be the night.

I played hard to get that night just a little longer every time he reaches for my panties I would move his hand and smile. Pushing him off me I got on top of him reach back and grabbed his dick, he was hard as a rock and I was wet as a water fountain. I played with his manhood for a minute then he got on top of me and took my panties off.

He pleased me that night I tried so hard not to be loud because his family was in the next room but I couldn't hold back he knew exactly what he was doing and very confident in the bedroom. It had felt like our private parts were meant to be connected to each stroke was filled with passion, the harder I threw it back it felt like his dick was in my stomach. At one point of time I wanted to cry because it felt so genuine, the way he touched me, looked me in my eyes while doing it was something I haven't felt since high school. Could this be my happy ending or what if he's just like the rest? what if he just wanted to have sex with me? what if he's the man for me? are all of the things that played in my head while making love to him then we both came.

"Oh shit what time is it?"

"12 O'clock why you gotta go?"

"Yes can you drop me off I really wish I could stay but I gotta be somewhere in the morning" He looked sad while putting on his clothes, my vagina was so swollen I needed to go home and soak so I lied. He wouldn't stop laughing as I was walking around his room trying to get my life together. My legs wouldn't stop shaking and I could barely walk when I tell y'all he laughed at me for so long all the way to my house until we got on the phone.

I was embarrassed like "What if he thinks I can't handle him? that was just a warm up next time I'm going to make him tap out". I woke up the next morning and I wasn't as soar as I was the night before.

"Good morning beautiful call me when you wake up" he had wrote in my inbox. I was still stuck, I finally got a good man that is excellent in bed.

Our time together was always great we joked and play fight a lot. One thing I never could get him to do was send his thingy to my phone, see me if you're mines I don't mind sending nudes I just needed something to look at while I played with myself when he was away.

"So you never sent a female your dick to their phone ever" looking me in my eyes he said

"No" once again I believed "my man" and left it alone. He began to get comfortable and would have me come over while leaving me in his room for hours while he go smoke with his brothers, I became annoyed. Bored so I decided to look through his computer where Facebook was left open ignoring that I went to his pictures on his computer and what do you know, dick pictures of him and naked females all through his computer.

I don't know if I was mad because they were all ugly females or because he lied over something so small. He came back in the room and I yelled

"Take me the fuck home!"

"What's wrong? what I do? please don't leave talk to me my love" his eyes watered as if he was about to cry then he walked to his computer and seen the pictures. I put on my clothes and continued telling him to take me home he dropped down to his knees and started crying begging me not to leave.

"Why did you lie to me? I don't care about the pictures it's the simple fact that you looked me in my eyes and you lied"

"How can you leave me without giving me a chance to explain myself?"

"Explain yourself then" I just knew whatever came out of his mouth was about to be another lie so I let him explain,

"Those are not my pictures I let my homeboy use my computer to back his phone up". I wanted to laugh in his face but it just made me madder.

"You mean to tell me these dick pictures in your computer is of someone else? another man dick is just sitting right here in your computer". First of all I know exactly how my man dick look so you not about to try to play me.

"Take me home and I'm not gonna ask you again!" he did as I said and dropped me off. Phone ringing as soon as he made it back home I ignored his call and laid there frustrated. See one thing about me is all it takes is one lie to make me look at you different because then I start thinking you're out to hurt me and I can't feel that pain again.

For The Worse

A couple days had passed and I had missed him and plus I was horny so I finally stopped ignoring him and let him come get me. We didn't talk about what had happened that night we just sat there watching movies in silence while sipping.

I caught a flashback and reach over and slapped his black & mild out his hand and it flew across the room. We laughed for so long he was mad as hell in the inside though.

"Oh you wanna play huh" tossing me on the bed while holding me down I laughed even harder while he pressed his manhood against my private. We had always use condoms this time we didn't he made love to me as if this was his way of apologizing knowing he had lied.

I began to scratch his back while telling him to go faster and faster then boom he nutted inside of me and laid there. In my head I was pissed like first of all you could have pulled out don't nobody want no baby right now but I just rolled over and caught my breath.

"We ain't done get your ass up matter fact catch your breath cause you gone need it. We rest for ten minutes then I got on top of him and rode him like I had never ridden any other man before.

His soul was mines. The way I fucked him I knew if we were to ever fall out our love would probably turn into hate.

I had loved him so much but was afraid of him hurting me. My family thought he was just the sweetest person ever because that was a side he would show them when he came around. Things were starting to change he would always have an attitude when we talked like I had done something to him when he was the one holding stuff back so instantly I got in defense mode and kept my guard up.

I stopped coming to his house for a few weeks and just stayed in my room and scrolled down my timeline or sometimes go chill with Chocolate.

He would post weird stats on facebook that made me feel uncomfortable and then pretend it came from a song. Different females coming out of nowhere all under his pictures but I never said nothing I would just pay attention carefully while waiting for the right moment to ask him about them even though I knew he was going to lie.

This nigga got me fucked up like I can't bounce back and get on my shit and let him know I don't need him. So I went and got my hair done and was instantly feeling myself. Posting a picture on Facebook he was the first one to comment under it trying to make it seem like everything was okay to the world when it wasn't. My phone started ringing

"Hello"

"What you doing my love you coming over?" much shit I talked about him I just couldn't stay away. He gave me a feeling that Sexy Face used to give me but better. 15 minutes later and he was outside in the car smoking them stank ass blacks.

"Now you wanna see me huh"

"Oh won't you stop" while smiling. I couldn't stand his fine ass.

"I gotta show you something when we make it to my house" We made it to his house and when I made it to his room there were pictures of me all over his mirror where Alicia Keys used to be. It made me smile I gave him a kiss and said

"Where the other bitch went?" we laughed he loved Alicia Keys so much I thought he would never take her down. It's like every time we were fucking she was just right there. We ended up fucking that night and as usual I made his lying ass take me home.

"Goodnight baby I'm tired I love you" a text from him had said. Dozing off I wake up to my phone ringing at 12 o'clock. It was my cousin girlfriend I can tell she was drunk and at the club because all I heard was loud music.

"Can you stay up and open the door for me I'm about to come there soon and oh your boyfriend here I was just talking to him". Wait hold up I know she didn't just say my man was at the club when he clearly told me he was going to sleep. Pissed off I hung the phone up and called and called and he didn't answer. He called me back an hour later telling me he was asleep I cussed him out so bad that night for lying and hung up on him.

I was at the end of the road with all of his lies. A year had passed and he just wouldn't stop lying to me. Maybe we weren't meant to be.

Bittersweet

Chapter 19

I remember back in high school dating people and getting them to fall in love with me knowing I couldn't catch them. I never knew how bad I was hurting people until I begin to feel the same way. Why was karma catching up to me now? I was beginning to do everything right and everything was still turning out wrong.

When I graduated high school I thought my love life would be easier but then I realized it was social media that was making it harder and harder for me to date.

I've been through so much from a kid to now so maybe I am good at pushing people away with my anger issues. It feels like I do everything right but the moment someone tries to play me that's when I turn into a different person and no longer care about your feelings.

It bothers me because people think I be the one doing things when in reality it be them. Somehow I still get blamed and judged.

Mr Unpredictable and I had became distant I was slowly walking away from him in silence. He was hurting me and treating me like I was average knowing he needed me.

A notification had went off on my phone from someone tagging me, it was a girl bringing up the rape situation that had happened between my man and his brothers and even though we weren't on talking terms I hopped right under that post and held him and his brothers down when I didn't have to. At the end of the day no matter what went on between me and him you don't throw dirt on peoples name. He was innocent we had the proof so I screenshot the letter and dropped it right under her comment, everyone shut up and apologized.

His brothers must of told him that I was real because he called me right after that saying thank you and that it meant a lot to him. We ended up talking and getting back together even though we had never actually broke up.

Thanksgiving was here and every year my family play football at the park so he came over and played with them. My best friend Pooh was staring him down that day he thought I didn't see him but I did. My best friend is one of those friends who is very over-protective. He don't want to see me hurting. I love him so much he reminds me of my cousin Sai. They talk alike, attitude alike, hoop alike and look just alike. People used to ask me why we never dated and maybe we would have made a cute couple but the love I have for him is so deep, I refuse to let a relationship come in between that. Everyone I date and everyone he dates always bring up each other's names, maybe because we are so close and no relationship can come in between me and him.

That day at the park was just to cute he was on homage. I didn't want my man to play because I didn't want him to get tackled to hard because I would have felt bad (laughing). He played really great though and I was proud of him just wish his ass would learn how to stop lying.

The more we had sex the more he would nut in me as if he was trying his hardest to get me pregnant but when I would tell him use a condom he would get upset. Maybe he felt it was almost the end of us and was trying to find a way to keep me in his life. The more I forgave him the more he lied and lied. He left his phone out and I went through his messages knowing I shouldn't have and there were messages from all the girls who naked pictures I had seen in his computer and girls I never even knew he dated. It would be like there messages then he would delete whatever he would send back.

∞∞∞

That was my last time putting my trust into him. I needed to clear my mind so I called Chocolate to come get me. Even after high school he always would listen to me when I needed to vent. We started spending a lot of time together even fucking on the regular but of course I was single. After all these years he still felt guilty for breaking my heart but always reminded me that I was a great woman and if he could rewind time he would.

Never Be The Same

Chapter 20

Today I woke up happy ready to get lit with my family, it was my aunty birthday and she had passed away so we always turn up for her that day and cook. I know that day always made Sai and Mario sad I hated when they were sad. They are the strongest men in the world. To lose your mom is a pain I don't want to experience but I know someday I am going to.

I couldn't waste anymore time on Mr Unpredictable so I continued my life without letting the internet in my business. I was heartbroken but I tried so hard not to let it bother me. He seemed okay but that's most men, quick to post but behind closed doors begging you back.

I spent the entire day with my family we partied all night. Sai was in the back room high as fuck. My ass was drunk, stumbling passed everyone I went to my room. An hour later Sai walked in

"Nana how I look? do I look cute? should I roll my sleeves up or wear them down?" while staring in my mirror.

"Oh shit you cute bitch where you going?" he started smiling so hard I had him feeling himself.

"My boys wanna go out tonight I don't really wanna go I just wanna stay home and finishing getting turnt for my mom birthday thurl".

Phone started ringing, I looked over and it was Mr Unpredictable calling. Rolling my eyes I ignored it and finished talking to Sai.

"You think you cute ole ugly self" he was still smiling, eyes about shut from smoking.

"Alrite I'm out thurl"

"Shut my door back bitch!" I yelled as he turned around and closed it.

∞∞∞∞

My head was spinning I had drank too much liquor and just wanted to sleep the rest of the night away so I closed my eyes. Three hours later my phone was ringing nonstop I assumed it was my ex calling so I didn't bother to look. My cousin Kieva yelled upstairs and I thought it was a dream.

"Nana Sai got stabbed at the club we gotta go to the hospital" I jumped out my sleep and sobered up so fast and put on my pajamas and rushed downstairs with tears rolling down my face.

"What happen? he was just here is he okay?" I asked.

"I don't know they said his friends were fighting and he tried to break it up and ended up getting stabbed". It felt like my heart had shattered into pieces.

Rushing out the house I get on Facebook and the internet was filled with stats about Sai. I couldn't believe this was happening, my phone wouldn't stop ringing but I didn't want to talk to anyone at the time. I looked in my messages and the first sentence was from a random girl that had said

"Your brother just got stabbed at the club I think he dead he's not moving at all" I got off Facebook and begin to pray in my head.

"God please just let him make it through this please that's all I'm asking". Walking into the hospital I needed answers I needed to know exactly what had happened. The emergency room was filled with all his friends that he had went to the club with everyone except for his best friend.

I stood there in shock it's like I was speechless for the first time ever, no words wouldn't come out just tears falling from my face. No one was giving us the answers that we need to know it's like they was holding information from us and playing dumb. They just kept saying they were fighting and Sai got stabbed when clearly y'all know who y'all were fighting. All I know is Sai better be okay.

A pastor had came and we all stood in a circle as he said a prayer. I cried even harder then I looked up in the look on my family face made it hurt even more. They were all broken, sad, confused, hurt I never seen that pain on any of their faces before. We waited in the lobby for answers and then the doctors came out,

"Are you the family of Saiquan Moore?"

"Yes" my aunt replied,

"Saiquan has lost a lot of blood and was in the cold for to long we are doing everything we can to stop the bleeding from his brain". He was stabbed a couple times as well as in his heart. Bursting out into tears I couldn't help but break down. Everyone kept asking where was his best friend but no one had answers I heard a few people saying they seen him leave with some girls. Calling his phone they finally got through to him

"Bruh it's not looking to well for Sai you gotta hurry and get to the hospital" hearing him from speaker phone say

"Nah bruh gonna be alright I'm with some hoes right now"

then he hung up the phone. Upset because out of everyone in this world they were together every second so I felt he should have been there but he wasn't.

Stay Strong

Chapter 21

The hospital was packed with people who cared about Sai and also nosy people who just wanted to see what was going on.

Facebook was depressing I had over a thousand friend request with hundreds of messages from people telling me to keep my head up. How can I keep my head up when the person I looked up to, made me feel safe and was always there for me was laying in a hospital bed fighting for his life?

I ended up sleeping in the chair that was there because there was no way I was leaving that hospital until I was told he was okay. A lot of my friends who I haven't seen since high school came to comfort me but out of everyone that came to that hospital it was this one moment I can never forget.

I remember I had my head down crying by myself and Asia from Freddie Thomas High School sat next to me even if it seemed as if I didn't want to be bothered. She took out a piece of tissue and wiped my face. Every tear that fell she caught them and that's something I can never forget. She didn't ask me was I ok she didn't tell me be strong she sat in silence and tried her best to keep the tears from falling. I never got the chance to tell her thank you but that moment meant everything to me.

All of my ex's was reaching out but I didn't care to reply, fuck y'all don't try to care for me now.

Seeing the tears in Mario face made my heart ache. It's like his soul had left his body. He looked angry and hurt. The next day his best friend had walked in and right before you know it a fist was coming across his jaw. I felt so bad because even though he didn't come the same day knowing he's the reason why Sai went out that night, that still was his best friend.

The tension in the room was thick. A lot of people were disappointed in him, including me but the love my cousin had for him I couldn't let that get in the way of what I was feeling. My male cousins felt otherwise and just wasn't with it, they wanted to fight everyone he had went out with that night. Shit they was punching everybody at the hospital even people who wasn't there. I'm like okay now y'all doing to much I understand y'all hurting but you don't take it out on innocent people.

I couldn't eat at all I was drained from crying, my phone was still ringing but I still didn't want to talk so I logged onto Facebook and said

"Thank you all for the love keep praying". I looked up in my ex was standing right there I was so pissed off like why are you even here? you don't even care for me all you ever did was lie to me. I yelled at him even though I was wrong I was still hurt for the way he was treating me and on top of that I was stressing about Sai. Deep down I was happy he came it's like I had mixed feelings.

"I've been calling you and calling you just to check on you but you won't answer and even though you might not wanna hear from me I just gotta be here for you" tears came down my eyes I wanted to believe that he really cared but I just couldn't so I told him to go home and that I would call him later. I knew I wasn't gonna call but I needed him to leave I didn't want to be around him.

Day two and nothing has changed so I put my head down and prayed again silently.

"Nana do you wanna go in the room and see him" my aunt asked, I didn't wanna see him like that but I needed him to hear my voice so I got up and walked in the room. As I made it to his bed he didn't look the same, that handsome face with that beautiful smile was gone, he was laying there breathless with tubes in his mouth. I wanted to die. I rubbed his arm and said

"Bra bra wassup dickhead? you gotta keep fighting because I need you, I need you to fight harder than you've ever fought before don't do me like this you can't leave me out here alone please I need you".

Before leaving the room I rubbed his arm once more and whispered I love you and walked out crying.

Walking back into the lobby I sat in the chair by myself turned on an instrumental and begin writing a song called "Stay Strong" because I wanted him to hear it when he had awaken.

Day 3

Day three of us sitting in the hospital the doctors had said he was doing better so I finally went home took a shower, grabbed my laptop and went to the studio before going back to the hospital.

My homeboy let me record at his studio because we all were best friends and hung together as kids so if it's anyone who knew my pain it was him. I played the beat and just knew I wasn't strong enough to record it but I needed to get it off my chest. He turned the lights off and let me zone out. I took a few shots and started recording, my voice cracked so I stopped rapping.

"Yo why you stop? that shit just gave me chills you gotta keep going"

"My voice keeps cracking I don't think I can do it" I told him.

"That's what makes it pure your pain, if you gotta cry while recording it's okay because it's your pain you gotta express yourself the way you know how if you wanna cry fuck that I'm right here with you".

He pressed record and I blacked out on the track, I let all my pain out and it felt good. After recording he grabbed me and we cried together as his voice played throughout the song then I made my way back to the hospital. Not really in the mood to talk to anyone so I put my headphones on and had the song I had just recorded on repeat.

∞ ∞ ∞

They had moved him to a different floor so I jumped on the elevator and when I made it there they were rushing him to a different elevator while blood was leaking from his bed, they couldn't stop the bleeding.

I bussed out crying along with everyone else, my faith was leaving but I needed to stay strong. I was beginning to panic. The tears wouldn't stop flowing and at that very moment I felt selfish. Selfish because I wanted him to fight for me so I wouldn't have to live the rest of my life hurting, but if fighting meant that it was hurting him I wanted the fight to be over.

Maybe heaven is where he belongs, maybe his mom needed him more than I did maybe god was taking him out of my life because of all the bad things I've done to people and how I treated people. Was this my karma?

Growing up I would wear his clothes when he left to play with his friends, wear all his jewelry and even put on his shoes and we didn't even wear the same size. He didn't know it but he was like a father to me, whenever someone made me cry he would come beat them up for me even if I was wrong.

He gave me money got on my damn nerves everyday but he had loved me so much. No matter how grown he was when night time came I would brush his hair and rub his ears until he fell asleep, that was our little thing. To the world he was a gangsta to me he was perfect he was my "Bra Bra" I've been calling him that since I was a kid because we lived together our whole life and was more like brothers and sisters.

My aunty raised us like siblings so all my cousins were really my brothers and sisters because we all lived under one roof.

Why god why? I needed answers. The time I spent in the hospital with my family, I thought it would bring us closer but it didn't, everyone argued every single day and I just didn't understand.

Taking some time to myself to respond to a few messages because I needed people to know that I was grateful for them reaching out I just wasn't thinking about the internet at the time.

"God if you hear me please don't take him away from me I can't make it without him, I don't think I'm strong enough but if you have to for your own reasons then I will understand". I prayed again in my head and sat down in the chair as time passed.

A couple hours later they were letting people see him a lot of faces I haven't seen in years. I don't think there was one time where I stopped crying, I remember standing there then my Chocolate walked in. I was shocked but he had known Sai before me. He gave me a warm hug and then walked in the room to show his respect. It made me feel bad that I had cussed Mr Unpredictable out but said nothing to Chocolate probably because we weren't on bad terms anymore and had squashed our differences a while back.

Mr Hood was out of jail and had reached out but I didn't get a chance to reply yet. After the night was slowing down I went home to rest.

Gone

Chapter 23

After the doctors had stopped the bleeding they told us he was doing better so I stayed home a little longer than I normally would. I needed the time alone while everyone was still at the hospital.

I sat in his room and prayed some more. Walking towards my room because my phone was ringing I hurried and answered, it was my cousin telling me to come quick the doctors had said he didn't have long to live. Confused and hurt I jumped up not realizing I'm home alone and don't have a ride out there I began to get frustrated. Mad at the world mad at myself and mostly mad at god. This can't be they told me he was doing better if I had known I would have never left the hospital.

My heart was beating so fast it felt like I had died. When I finally got there everyone was staring at me with this sad look on there face. My aunty looked at me and said

"He's gone" I screamed and ran out of the hospital and broke down outside. Harvey which is another one of Sai best friends held me and I cried and cried and cried. My heart was hurting in a way it never had felt before. My phone was going off, everyone wanted to know was it true did he pass away. My cousin Kiamesha inbox me and said

"I know these questions are annoying you by now but I just don't understand is he still with us or with god?" I responded

"He's with god" she said

"He was fighting Nana it took days until it came to this. I'm sorry, though I know you're hurting I dropped tears, I know what that pain feels like when it hits home it feels like it hurts the most, try to stay strong, I know it's easy to say until we all meet again".

I slowly walked back inside the hospital towards the elevators. My head was spinning it felt like I was about to pass out. Entering his room everyone surrounded his bed, they had told me right before he passed away a tear rolled down his face and it made me cry harder.

I made my way through everyone and held his hand, closed my eyes and said

"Why did you leave me like this? I needed you, but you're no longer in pain tell aunty I said hi and don't worry about your friends and family I would keep everyone together I love you until we meet again Bra Bra".

The pastor had everyone hold hands while we said one last prayer as the doctors unplugged the machines he was hooked to.

Mario made it there last he didn't want to believe that his brother was gone. It was hard for him to come say goodbye.

That very same day I knew life was turning for the worse I knew I would never be the same. Mr Unpredictable was calling me non-stop but I wasn't in the mood to talk.

His basketball coaches reach out and I told them that Sai had passed and they cried. Coach Nash was like a father to Sai even funnier because they looked alike.

Coach Binion was like another father as well he was there since we were kids playing basketball at the Rec center giving him hell so I knew it hurt him just as deep.

We ended up staying at the hospital as long as we could until they took his body away. Walking into the house my breaths got shorter and the tears fell harder, I walked passed his room then walked in mine, turned the music as loud as I could and cried like a baby. Everyone was in the living room drinking, crying and sharing memories.

He never got to hear the song that I made for him which broke my heart so I walked downstairs and played it for them. Everyone listened to the words carefully and cried as I cried while playing the song and right at the end of the song Sai voice said "

 "This ya boy Sai man if I ain't here to uh pick your call up just hit me back you already know Scio City".

My family looked at me with a shocked but happy look like wow you got his voice on this song. They played that song over and over and over. I went to my room and uploaded it to Soundcloud so my Facebook friends could hear it and they went crazy.

The Wake

Chapter 24

"I'm sorry Booka I wish I was there to hold you I know how you feeling I just went through it keep your head up if you need anything I'm here".

Mr Hood had wrote on my wall, one of his close friends had just passed away and I didn't get a chance to reach out to him so I knew he was still going through it. Sai and him would always drill each other in school.

People I've never seen or ever spoke to in Rochester was reaching out but if they were friends of Sai I made a promise to him that I would be there.

Right before the wake I sat down and tried my best to respond to everyone's messages. Impossible because they were coming to my inbox nonstop but I still tried.

Getting dressed not knowing was I ready to see him again so I took my time. Everyone was already at the wake already. I don't remember how I got there but I made it. When I arrived I barely could get in, he was loved the parking lot was packed people were blasting they music, drinking, taking pictures, crying and most of all showing love.

I walked towards the casket and broke down. I wanted to switch places with him I wanted to know what really happened that night, feeling weak while trying to hold it together an arm touch me.

Looking up it was my dad with his arms out he grabbed me laid my head on his chest and held me as I cried, I probably cried for about 20 minutes. My dad was there for me and it felt so good to feel his touch. His eyes were red from crying he loved Sai so much he used to call him "Early Man" because he said ever since Sai was a kid he always looked like a grown man.

Walking away from the casket I sat three rolls down and just stared at his body while everyone broke down and cried as they walked to view his body. All of the teachers from Freddie Thomas came and showed love including Mr Morgan. He thought me and Sai was the coolest people in the world he used to say

"You guys have so much gear" so when he walked in with his black clothing on because he was one of them white cool teachers I laughed to myself and stood up and gave him a hug.

A loud cry came from the other end of the room it was his basketball coach he walked to the casket holding his basketball jersey number two, placed it inside and cried as he touched his body.

Everyone in the room started crying it was painful to watch. Our eyes had connected then he walked over to me and held me tight as we both cried he said

"Sai was like another son to me if you ever need anything you come to me I want you to come up to Freddie Thomas Monday morning I got something for you" then he walked away.

"Yo Nana they fighting outside someone just punched his best friend in the face".

Rushing outside I was pissed because no matter what that was still Sai best friend and he would kill for him. I promised Sai that his friends would be okay so I went out looking for him.

He was nowhere to be found asking around a female said they had seen him down the street in an alley. I walked until I seen him, he was sitting by himself crying it broke me down he told me what had happened and I became angry.

"Man fuck these niggas you made a mistake by not being there but you're here now I got you come on we walking back and you're going to see Sai". Hesitant at first but he followed behind me.

Everyone looked at us as if he wasn't supposed to be there. It was so many people they weren't trying to let us in I told them to go get my aunty. She came to the door and they let us in.

He cried all the way to the casket and broke down when he made it to the front. I felt his pain, they were best friends, together every single day if you see one the other one was right there. His body looked drained I grabbed him while he cried to comfort him and everyone gathered around him while he cried then shots fired off.

They were outside shooting so my aunty made them shut the wake down early. A lot of people didn't get to view his body which wasn't our fault. It took about two hours to clear the inside of the wake and the outside parking lot. My aunty and my cousins got in the car I tried to slide my little ass in but it wasn't no room.

"Ain't that bout a bitch" they all started laughing.

"We gone come back and get you" my cousin Kieva said.

"Nah I'm just playing I'm good I'll meet y'all home I know damn near everyone out here someone gone take me".

They pulled off and I jumped in the car with one of my cousins.

Riding down the street I see a boy in the middle of the street with something in his hand. Pulling up closer it was my cousin.

"Yo what's wrong? man get in the car"

"Nah Nana they took my nigga somebody gotta die tonight fuck that they gotta feel my pain".

He looked hurt and angry and I knew no matter what I had said he wasn't going to listen to me so I told him be safe and pulled off.

∞∞∞

Making it to the house cars parked everywhere even in the grass. My first thought was if any of these ugly muthafuckas in my room everybody getting kicked out.

I walked through the front door and said wassup to everyone then walked upstairs. Friends from high school I haven't seen in forever was standing in the hallway

"Excuse me" I walked in my room it was liquor spilled all over my brand new rugs. I had just remodeled my room and was waiting for my bed to come so I had an air mattress at the time. Before I could cuss out everyone I looked down and seen my dad sitting on my bed with his head down with tears in his face drinking a bottle of Remy. It was so many people on that little ass air mattress all of the air had left I couldn't do anything but laugh they literally was sitting on the floor. Mario looked at me and said

"Wassup sis you alright?" and at that moment I said fuck this room if Mario is smiling then I'm happy.

"I was about to fuck y'all up but ima let you slide" while smiling at him. He folded the air mattress up so that more people can enter the room.

Blasting Future "ring ring" was one of Sai favorite songs, everyone danced and jumped up and down I thought they were going to fall through the ceiling.

Walking into his room where it was packed as well I spoke to everyone took pictures and finished drinking.

Next they played his other song he liked Rick Ross "Stay Schemin" everyone got hype all you heard was "Hudson" then boom everyone starts fighting the guy.

The females ran out the house my room was so packed I couldn't do nothing but run in my closest in shut the door. While peeking out I looked at the guy and he was bloody they tried to throw him out the window. When he finally got up he had blood everywhere and it scared the shit out of everyone so they ran away from towards him. His ass looked like a monster or some shit. Looking around my room seeing blood everywhere all over my new clothes, rugs, my mirrors were all broken and everything in my room was damaged.

I was pissed I had nowhere to sleep while everyone else was going home to a comfortable clean house. Next minute you know the police came rushing upstairs making everyone come down. Females were crying because they were scared Mario yelled

"Man if y'all don't shut yo ass up" I laughed so loud when he said that because we from the hood we used to the police messing with us but they weren't.

The twins K-naste and Tierra were right there they never left my side. We made it outside and they made everyone walk to the corner. It was freezing that night.

Me and the twins was in the corner hugging trying to keep each other warm. The day was so long I couldn't even cry no more I just laughed to myself like this can't be happening.

Mario was wasted he started cursing the police out

"My fucking brother is gone and y'all got us standing at this fucking corner in the cold like we done something wrong fuck y'all" he was hurting and his emotions started pouring out.

After they checked the house for weapons and didn't find anything they let us go back home. My friends asked did I need somewhere to stay I told them I'm good, gave them hug and we parted
ways.

My room was fucked so I called my ex Mr Unpredictable
knowing he would come and told him to come get me and he
came. Taking me back to his house, I sat there in silence and he
held me until I fell asleep.

Heal

Life after a death never gets easy. When Sai passed away I cried everyday after the funeral, my body was feeling lifeless and I started losing weight. They say everything happens for a reason a man had inboxed me and said

"I'm sorry for what my son did I'm trying to make him turn himself in please forgive me". I told my family what he had said but nobody did anything.

Me and my family partied everyday and drank liquor to hide our pain. Everyone tried to be strong for each other but deep down pain was filled within.

I knew my mom was hurting but she did so well at holding it in and staying strong for the family. Whenever my aunty would drink it hurt my heart so much to see her cry because I was so used to seeing her laughing, or cussing someone out.

She took care of a lot of people here in Rochester Ny. No one in this world can speak bad about her no matter how mean she may appear to be her heart was solid.

We were all under one roof together and happy. I remember I would cry and run to her whenever it was time to go home because I wanted to stay with her and be with all of my other cousins. Hammer, Shep, Sai, Kieva & Mario them were the cousins I wanted to be around.

Being that I was an only child at the time made it hard to be away from them.

Mario and Shep were older so mainly Hammer, Kieva and Sai even though they were all mean to me. I remember they would make fun of my gap and call my gums "dookie gums" because they weren't pink like theirs. I would run outside sit by the garbage and just cry. I hated my smile I hated my gums so whenever I went to school I would smile with my mouth closed. Maybe they were being mean to me because I was the youngest or maybe I was really ugly to them who knows.

Although we were young they made me feel like I wasn't good enough because no one wanted to hang with me but then I realized they didn't wanna hang with me because I told on every little thing they did.

My aunty raised us like siblings she even let me move in with her and live rent free when she didn't have to. Appreciated and grateful no matter what is something I would always feel when it comes to her. My second mom, I love her equally as my real mom because whenever the special moments happened in my life like birthdays, Christmas, or even needing a band aid she was there.

Thank you for everything, you taught us that family is important and to always protect each other.

Now that Sai is gone it hurts more because all of our memories are with each other.

My cousin Shep was in jail at the time so he didn't get to say goodbye to Sai so I knew when he came home that pain would still be there.

Hammer and Sai were more like twins the same age and always dressed alike as kids so I knew his heart wouldn't be the same either.

My cousin Kieva is the mean cousin that just don't like no one (laughing) and whatever she says goes. The boys always got on her nerves and although she plays tough I knew the heart she had was the same as her moms. When she tells us something I always knew it was for the better even when it comes to our relationships.

Sai death brought us closer but only us, the rest of the family had changed for the worse.

After the funeral one of my toxic cousins had taken Sai car and wouldn't give it to us after his brother was asking for it then months later his car magically disappeared. I felt bad because that could have been something that his brother could have cherished.

I have three toxic cousins and she's the one I dislike the most but that's another chapter you'll hear about later.

How do I cope with death? is a question a lot of you asked me and still ask me. Prayer, it took a lot of prayer and forgiveness to feel at ease because the pain never really goes away. I had to forgive the person who killed him I had to forgive God for taking him away from me and more importantly I had to forgive Sai for choosing heaven over earth.

It's okay to cry, sometimes crying makes you feel better I had lost myself when I lost Sai and I needed help. The liquor wasn't working anymore it just made me sadder and madder so I stopped drinking, and fell back from relationships.

I even apologized to Mr Unpredictable even though we were already apart I just couldn't love him even though I wanted to. He was angry but if he cared like he said he did he would understand.

This chapter is for everyone who has ever lost someone close to them step one, cherish every moment that you spend with the people you love because you never know when it would be your last time with them. Step two forgive if you don't forgive those who do wrong your heart will become bitter and step three **LIVE**. The reason why I say live is because we spend to much time being alive but not really living. Get out and have fun, spend your time with your family and friends and stop focusing on the past.

Unforgettable

2012

Chapter 26

After time had passed Sexy Face would find ways to pop up in my life. He must of found out I was back single but he had hurt me so bad through the years to where I had finally really moved on. I got so used to his ways I knew exactly how to deal with him.

Me and Unpredictable were apart for a year after he showed his ass on social media and that very same day I told myself I could never love another man he even left a disrespectful voicemail on my phone that hurt me more than his actions did.

I took my Facebook down for a couple months and started using my Twitter account more. It was hard to get used to Twitter like I had got used to Facebook but I had so many famous people following me such as Cassidy, Joe Budden and a few others.

"Hey I like your tweets you're so wise" a girl that I had never seen a day in my life had written on my page.

"Thank you I appreciate it" I replied then going to her page to follow her back.

Sexy Face was still working overnights at the gym so he would text me around four in the morning asking for a quickie. Bad as he wanted it I did to so if he thought he was coming back to use me for sex I was really using him.

I had learned how to separate my feelings and only came around when I wanted sex from him.

We would ride around for twenty minutes looking for somewhere to fuck, most times we didn't care where we parked.

One time we did it in front of someone's house we were so horny we couldn't do nothing but laugh. Friends with benefits were definitely our title. He wasn't shit but always satisfied me when it came to sex and was still fine as ever the more he came around.

The girl from Twitter would message me saying we should text but I wasn't really into making friends so I would just ignore her. Up late nights tweeting

   "Can't wait until he gets off work and come get me because I'm drunk and horny". A lot of people were usually up around that time tweeting the same thing but it felt like every time I would post about him the random girl tweets referred to mines.

Maybe I was tripping because she didn't know me and I didn't know her but still she would reach out and tell me we should be friends so I finally texted her.

She was a very sweet girl we would text each other good morning goodnight you know normal stuff until one day we finally met in person.

I was shy because I didn't know her like that so I didn't know what the hell we would talk about. Getting into her car we spoke to each other and she told me about the problems she was having with this guy and I told her the problems I was having.

We talked for hours and watched tv as she kept her car on the whole time. The more we talked the more I felt I had finally found another female friend who I can finally trust.

"I gotta tell you a secret" she had texted me one day. I was scared and didn't wanna know but I still responded

"Wassup?"

"There's this person I like and I don't know how to tell them". Apart of me felt like she was talking about me but then again we both were into men so hell I didn't know what was going on. I told her if she had liked that person then maybe she should go for it not knowing if she would take my advice.

A couple weeks later she randomly text

"You should be my girlfriend" I swear my heart was in my ass because first of all I'm not gay at all but still my scary ass responded

"Well okay". It was funny because she had said we didn't have to have sex or anything and boy was I happy and dumb for believing that.

In my head I thought we would just be real cool, hang out, talk something like fake girlfriends but the more we came around one another feelings were starting to grow.

It was weird to me because I never liked a female before and I damn sure don't plan on having sex with one.

Slow music and long talks was our thing for months just having company around felt good.

Months passed by and I had loved her but of course I wasn't going to tell her that.

She invited me over to her house one day, it was a nice little drive and nothing like what I was used to. I can tell it was a nice area where probably only white folks lived. In my head I'm like this girl gotta be rich her house looked like a mansion I felt like T.I when he first found out who New New really was (laughing).

Walking into her home she lead me downstairs and turned on slow music while she took a shower. The mood was perfect for us to relax and bond with one another. When I heard the shower water stop I was happy because I had missed her that fast.

She came out of the bathroom with these small shorts on and boy was she looking good. I didn't know rather to close my eyes or pretend something was in them.

Why is she doing this to me? I felt like she was teasing me, she knew she was very attractive because she came out of the bathroom smiling.

Sitting there nervously with my hat on she came walking towards me and sat on my lap and started tongue kissing me. Her lips were so soft and she kissed so much better than men. I sat back and she followed and continued kissing me while I slowly moved my hands to her waist. Not knowing what the hell I was doing but it sure felt great. The more I kissed her soft moans escaped from her mouth. She reached down and unzipped my pants I was more wetter than I've ever been.

In my head I'm like

"Bitch I thought we ain't have to have sex" (laughing) but I wanted it I just didn't know what the hell I was doing.

Following her every move while taking each other's clothes off nervously I insert my finger insider her while she bit down on my neck. Next she got on top of me and kissed on my stomach all the way to my thighs. I was more confused than I've ever been in life, I didn't know what the hell was happening but the butterflies felt real.

Feeling her tongue against my pussy gave me a different kind of feel as if my vagina had a heart beat. I'm like

"Oh shit does this make me gay because I don't wanna be gay". I loved men too much. I came all over her face and she motioned herself on her back while pulling me down to kiss her.

I guess it was my turn to return the favor I was clueless so I tried remembering her every move she demonstrated on me.

every time I kissed on her body I thought to myself

"This is really gay as fuck" but I kept going. Sucking on her breast while playing with her pussy was making her moan louder and louder so I knew I had to be doing something right, well for now. Her breast were so beautiful I sucked on them for a minute while taking my time because I was scared to go any further.

I glanced up and her head was tilted back while biting her bottom lip I started moving lower and lower.

Kissing between her thighs softly I made my way to her vagina and gently kissed it.

"Welp! bitch this is it you might as well gone finish you already down here" is what I had told myself while laughing in my head. Sticking my tongue inside her a moan escaped from her mouth.

Damn she tastes good I rotated my tongue over and over around her clit because I just knew that's what always felt good to me.

She was getting wetter and wetter while repeating the words "Fuck" over and over.

One thing's for sure no one is about to cum in my mouth not even a man will ever be able to so I jumped up quick as fuck and pretended as I was tired.

Tongue kissing me some more she rolled over while smiling and said

"Was it gross to you?" I laughed

"No I just can't believe I had sex with a female but I liked it" then we heard a noise upstairs.

It was her parents I was scared as hell we jumped up quick and got dressed she told me to wait downstairs. All types of thoughts ran through my head like do her parents know about me? do they know she like females? and afraid they would ask me questions I didn't know the answers to.

I heard someone walking down the stairs it was her dad, oh shit fake sleep nah that obvious just sit here and stare at the TV that haven't been turned on since I got here.

"Hello" he looked at me and said

"How you doing sir?" I replied.

"Darling is the tv not working for you still" he yelled upstairs

"No dad something wrong with it, so we just decided to listen to music instead". He walked towards the tv and started touching it but it still wouldn't work so he went back upstairs.

My ass was scared and ready to go she walked back downstairs while smiling then sat next to me.

"My mom don't really like me with girls so when we leave she might question you". See dads be calm but people's moms on the other hands always scared the hell out of me.

"Oh my god this is my song you heard this before"

"Nah who that?" I asked

"Girl Boyz II Men it's called Four Seasons Of Loneliness this song gives me life."

I listened to the words carefully and Sexy Face came across my mind, the song had reminded me of him.

She started singing, her voice was so beautiful I didn't know she can sing that great then she shyly looked away. I put my hand on her thigh and smiled at her without making too much eye contact.

"Tonight was wonderful. I really enjoyed every moment and I hope you did as well" before I could respond she said

"Shut up they playing my other jam" I laughed because I loved the way she talked she was one of those black girls who acts all the way white and it turned me on even more.

"Girl this song helped me get through so many hard times it's called "Just Fine" by Boyz II Men". She started singing again and I fell in love with the words that were being sung.

No good ass Sexy Face popped back up in my head I just wanted him out my brain.

After the song went off she asked was I ready to go home and I said yeah while trying to hurry before her mom catch us leaving. We ran right into her

"How you doing?" I said while walking towards the door she smiled and spoke back while yelling something to her daughter.

Driving off still shocked that I had just lost my female virginity I smiled the whole ride home while listening to her sing.

We pulled up in front of my house and talked for a bit before I went inside.

"Text me so I can know you made it home safe"

"Ok baby" while leaning over to give me a kiss. I damn near died because my family didn't know what the hell was going on and my aunt always peeking out the window. I kissed her fast and ran in the house. My auntie was in the bathroom boy was I happy.

I walked into my room grabbed my towel took a shower and laid down while waiting for her text. I dead ass just ate pussy kept playing in my brain.

"I'm home baby and I miss you, what are you doing?" I loved the way she text she always spelled everything out.

"Just got out the shower missing you as well tonight was amazing".

"Please don't be scared when I tell you this but I love you and if you don't feel the same way right now it's ok". My heart dropped when I saw those words come across my screen. I was afraid of love but I knew deep down I had loved her too so I replied

"It's ok because I love you too and I'm here for you. At that moment I knew I had to stop the back and forth with Sexy Face because I didn't want to hurt her.

Signs

The more time we spent together the more I was falling in love with her. Can't believe after all these years of saying I would never date a female here I am in love with one.

"I wanna see you babe where are you?"

"I'm at the gym playing basketball baby I'll be home in a few hours". I was thirsty to get home I played a few games and called her after I made it home and showered. I walked outside and sat and just before I could hug her my aunty swung the door open and said

∞∞∞∞

"This girl been coming down here every single day and parking in that same damn spot get out the car and come speak to me". Holy fuck my aunt plays to much she got out the car and we walked towards the door.

"You a pretty little thing how you doing baby?" I knew my aunty was drinking because she's never actually this nice. They talked for a minute then my aunty invited her to her birthday gathering that was coming up the following weekend.

"Ok now I just wanted to see the pretty little lady who always park her car outside my house and never come in" we laughed and I shook my head while walking back into the car.

Your aunt is funny I like her how was the gym?"

"The gym was pretty cool I missed you though".

"I missed you more baby that's why I wanted to see you and I gotta talk to you about something".

Afraid because when people say they gotta talk to you about something it always be something you rather not hear.

She pulled out a piece of paper and handed it to me. I read it while my eyes got watery and at the bottom was a picture she had drawn of a treasure chest that had said

"Your secrets are safe with me". I smiled no one has ever done something so sweet like this before.

"Why you tryna make me cry? you're so amazing"

"I was thinking about you all day and I like to write so I decided to write you a letter".

"I gotta talk to you don't be mad at me but the guy that I keep telling you about that hurt me was the same guy you were dating, now before you get upset just promise me you won't go back to him".

When she said his name I wanted to die it was Sexy Face the guy I've loved since 7th grade, the guy that broke my heart over and over and over and now this is the mystery female he was playing me with all along. I couldn't believe it.

"Why didn't you tell me this? come on man that's crazy like I feel like you played me" she looked sad while explaining herself she told me that she knew who I was all along and that she didn't plan for all this to happen. It was to late we were in love and didn't know what was next.

"First of all I do not want that clown back all we do is fuck and that's about it." We promised each other that we would cut him off and continue our relationship even though I felt betrayed.

"I really love you Nana I didn't plan on falling in love with you but I did and I don't wanna lose you especially over him he's been playing both of us". Her voice always did something to me she always sounded so innocent and sincere so I took her word for it.

"I really like this treasure chest though ima get it tattooed on me watch"

"Ima get it to it can symbolize us and only we will know what it stands for" that very same day we promised each other that from here on out it would always be us.

Not really in the mood to talk any longer I told her I was a little tired and wanted to rest she seemed sad because she probably knew I was bothered but I didn't care I hugged her gave her kiss and walked in the house.

She sat outside for a second before pulling off. I laid in bed and went to his text messages I wanted to curse him out so bad that day but instead I deleted everything while tears ran down my face.

 High school memories played in my head over and over I knew this girl face from somewhere but I couldn't think where from so I went through my pictures from school that a friend had given me.

My heart dropped, there she was in the background of a picture I remember seeing him in on prom day spraying something on his hair that looked like oil sheen wearing a pink shirt. I stared at the picture for five minutes because I couldn't believe it.

I'm dating the girl that he's been cheating on me with through-out our whole relationship. I couldn't do nothing but cry I wanted to breakup with her for not telling me ahead of time but it was to late I had loved her.

It all started playing in my head from the time I caught him in the hallway on the phone while rushing to hang up when he saw that I had seen him to the time I went through his phone and seen messages between them all the way until the prom picture.

I finally met the girl who's been in the picture this whole time. I was hurt all over again I hated him all over again, that same feeling that I had finally thought I let go in high school had came back.

Chemistry

"**B**estie what you doing? I have been on the block all night I need to come over and take a nap"

The door unlocked just come over".

My best friend and I were very close he loves me to death and I love him to death. That's my heart whenever he would come over I would pray for him while he's asleep. When I look at him I see Sai. Same attitude same face it's scary.

"What have you been up to pussy?" he always like talking shit to me that's just how we've been since kids. I wasn't ready to tell him I was out here eating pussy so I just smiled and said

"Just tryna stay out the way bestie". My phone started ringing it was Sexy Face I ignored him and laid down beside my bestie and we fell asleep.

When we woke up we decided to play 2k we always went at it. Spending time with him always meant a lot because that way I knew he was safe.

"Bestie I gotta catch a lick ima holla at you later". When he left I got up and went on Facebook and went on "Her" page I called her "My 4" four means love. She was my love despite the things we were going through I still loved her.

∞∞∞

 Staring at her profile picture she was fine as hell she had on these shades with her hair long and straight while making this cute smirk.

 Reading her stats I can tell she was feeling me I never clicked like on really anything because people are nosy and I'm sure she was watching my page all day as well.

All her friends wanted to know who was this mystery person making her happy and all my friends wanted to know who was making me happy. They kept saying stuff like who is this lucky man? shit little do they know it's a whole female.

I haven't had a tattoo in a while so I called up my tattoo artist and told him I need a tattoo today. Treasure chest was the first thing that came to my mind so I took out the picture she made and walked down to his house.

 "Hey babe" It was My 4 texting me so I pretended I was still at home so she wouldn't know that I was gonna surprise her with the tattoo when I seen her today.

My body was covered in tattoos so I didn't know where to get it, so I decided to get it on my left arm almost by my elbow. I was so excited to show her.

She ended up coming over that night and we talked for a while then I removed my jacket and showed her. Her face lit up, she couldn't believe that I had really did it. Shit I didn't think I was really gonna do it because sometimes I just be talking but I actually did it then I posted the picture on Facebook.

Later that night we ended up laying up and watching tv which turned to us fucking as usual. It was something about her, she was addicted to me and I was addicted to her. We fucked every time we were around each other. The more we did it the better I became.

We would subtweet all day on Twitter about one another while trying to keep it a secret. Eventually it felt like people were catching on to us because we would use the term "bestie".

Together every single day laughing and sipping I was happy and it was all because of a female.

"Wanna go bowling?" I love bowling so when she asked me to go I was excited. She came and got me later on that night and called my phone when she was outside.

"Wassup baby?"

"Hi baby" we talked and sipped our liquor the whole time until we made it to the bowling alley.

We were having a ball our first time really out in public and plus I was tipsy. I seen a few familiar faces that went to high school with me and the girl I was about to fight at the beach she was cool with my ex so deep down I figured she would tell him I was there.

In my mind I said if she close to him she must know this is his ex as well.

My turn to bowl and I kept catching her look our way and what do you know his corny ass came walking right through the bowling alley. I laughed so hard because I know he felt stupid and caught up.

"What is going on here? what is this?" he asked while I continued to laugh. It was her turn to bowl he looked at me and asked again so I snapped and said

"Boy if you don't get the fuck on I don't even know why she

called you here". When Sexy Face was bothered it showed all in his face and I was loving it.

He then asked her what was going on and why were we hanging together she looked afraid as I paid attention to her body language. He stood there for about ten minutes and when he realized I was still laughing and his questions wasn't being answered he walked out the bowling alley.

Looking back while his "friend, sister" whatever you wanna call her was staring our way I shook my head at her and continued bowling even though we both wasn't in the mood anymore.

Still following her body language I can tell she was ready to go so I grabbed our stuff and we left.

   "That's mad corny to me I knew she was going to call him and let him know we were at the bowling alley".

I finished the rest of my liquor that I had left in the car. My whole mood had changed we made it back to my house and sat in the car and talked for a couple hours, we usually would have went upstairs but this time she went home.

Maybe this was too much for her but she should have known this would happen being that we dated the same person and we all lived in Rochester Ny where it's very small here.

I didn't know if this situation would bring us closer now that he saw us in person or would it change for the worse.

I Should Have Known

After the bowling situation we decided to leave it alone and continued focusing on us.

She had been searching for apartments for months and finally had got approved I was happy for her. I was in love with her apartment and her living room was so beautiful.

"You should stay the night with me"

"Aiight when I leave the studio you can come get me". The studio was like an everyday thing for me even if I wasn't going down there to rap. I would sit there and drink with my big brother while he record other artists or I would watch him edit music videos.

Exclusive was our drink it always made us get drunk fast then next minute you know we up dancing listening to Dru Hill.

It used to feel weird because usually when I was there it would be me and my homegirls but now it was just me and I wasn't ready to tell my brother I was dating a female but he probably knew already.

"He keep texting me asking about us" I read my girlfriend text and instantly became angry.

"Why does he still text and call you? do you want him back

or something because you be seeming bothered" the liquor had kicked in which made it easier to say what was on my mind.

"No I don't want him back I didn't even respond to his message" ignoring her text I continued drinking even more by that time I was horny.

"Nana" What are you doing? why are you not responding? I'm about to come get you.

Shit I was drunk and my brother had left out the studio for a bit so I told her to come get me. She pulled up ten minutes later because she had lived closer now.

"You were drinking weren't you"

"Hell yeah" she laughed and said

"I can tell". I was hungry as hell and my head was spinning.

"My best friend coming over I'm gonna cook for us okay" I was happy when she said cook because I was starving.

We made it to the house I took off my shoes and sat on the couch. Damn she looked good I loved staring at her especially watching her cook.

I was so drunk I moved from the couch and sat on the floor with my hat over my face. A knock at the door scared the shit out of me it was her best friend.

"Hello" she said

"This crazy girl done got drunk "I looked up and smiled then I spoke back.

"Huh bae eat this for now you need something in your stomach". She passed me some pasta that I never had tried before but when I tasted it I fell in love with it. I got in the shower while she finished cooking.

The liquor was wearing off but I still was horny and I knew her friend wasn't leaving no time soon so I walked in the room and laid down then five minutes later they followed behind me.

She put on a movie and we sat there and watched it then her best friend asked did she have something to drink as she walked to the kitchen. When she came back she had a big bowl of pasta and my girlfriend looked at her and said

"Well damn bitch did you get enough?" in the inside I died laughing but I mind my business and laid there. It was so funny to me I couldn't do nothing but pick up my phone and text her while she was laying next to me.

"Really bae you had to say all that" then we laughed out loud.

After the movie was over her best friend had left and she turned on "Martin". Rubbing my hands passionately across her butt I made my way to her breast while sticking my tongue down her throat. We both started breathing heavily while undressing each other next minute you know we were laying there butt ass naked.

"Can we 69 tonight?" while looking at me smiling

"Yeah baby". She bent down and placed her ass in the air I was nervous because we had never done that before but I knew I had wanted to.

I heard my phone ringing but there was no way I was bout to stop and answer it. By that time I felt her lips rub across my clit so I lined my body up with hers while eating her from the back. She moaned

"Fuck!" so loud it scared me I thought I had accidentally bit her or something but I guess not because she got louder and louder while her legs started shaking.

It felt so good pleasing each other at the same time I could taste her cummin over and over after saying I wouldn't let anyone cum in my mouth.

Every time a freaky song came on it makes us keep going longer and longer until we both collapsed and laid there still in the same position. Damn that was good the bed was soaking wet we just looked at each other and smiled while we held each other until we fell asleep. The next day she dropped me off at home and soon as I made it in the house she texted me

"Um"

"Um what baby?"

"You were down there as I was…." I licked my lips and replied

"I know baby"

"But you said you weren't going to be down there when I was cummin". I couldn't do nothing but laugh because I remember saying I wasn't going to let her cum in my mouth but I did I guess my sex game was getting more intense than I thought.

All summer we would go to the liquor store go catch a movie or just chill at the park and sip. Everywhere I went she was right there with me. A couple weeks later that's when I got a text that had said we need to talk. Every time she said we need to talk I knew it was something serious.

"I'm sorry but me and my ex is getting back together and he's moving in with me". At that moment I thought my world was ending.

www.ingramcontent.com/pod-product-compliance
Lightning Source LLC
Chambersburg PA
CBHW030639130626
46552CB00002B/936